PHANTOM of
BLOOD ALLEY

PAUL STEWART & CHRIS RIDDELL

PHANTOM of BLOOD ALLEY

Illustrated by Chris Riddell

CORGI BOOKS

BARNABY GRIMES: PHANTOM OF BLOOD ALLEY
A CORGI BOOK 978 0 552 55627 9

First published in Great Britain by Doubleday,
an imprint of Random House Children's Books
A Random House Group Company

Doubleday edition published 2009
Corgi edition published 2010

1 3 5 7 9 10 8 6 4 2

Set in Aldus

Corgi Books are published by Random House Children's Books,
61–63 Uxbridge Road, London W5 5SA

www.kidsatrandomhouse.co.uk
www.rbooks.co.uk

Addresses for companies within The Random House Group Limited can be found at:
www.randomhouse.co.uk/offices.htm

THE RANDOM HOUSE GROUP Limited Reg. No. 954009

A CIP catalogue record for this book is available from the British Library.

Printed in the UK by CPI Bookmarque, Croydon, CR0 4TD

For Clare

CHAPTER 1

'I have suffered the torments of hell,' whispered the phantom. 'Now it is your turn, Barnaby Grimes.'

The pungent stench of sea-coal smoke and scorched chemicals made my eyes water and caught in my throat. There were splashes of a thick, viscous liquid on the floor at my feet, and the ornate brass gas lamp which jutted from the wall was ablaze.

A length of crimson silk had been wrapped round the lamp's mantle and glass cowl. It dulled the glare of the gaslight, its muted light casting the whole room in a hellish red glow. It shone on the low, flaking ceiling, on the planks of wood nailed across the single window, and on rows of portraits pinned to the walls and hanging from the clothes line above my head.

There were men and women. Old and young. A scrivener with a long quill and inky fingers. A butcher in a spattered apron with a dead rabbit raised in one hand. A milkmaid, a river-tough, a chimney-sweep's young lad . . . They all gazed down at me in that crimson light, like the lost souls of the damned.

To my left, a splintered bench ran the length of the room, a sink at its centre and three large zinc trays beside it. Shelves, bowing under the weight of glass bottles of dark chemicals and glittering powders, lined the wall above it. To my right were two worm-eaten cupboards and a rickety table, its warped top overflowing with equipment. Scalpels, shears and a paper guillotine; bottles of ink and goosefeather quills; a magnifying

They all gazed down at me in that crimson light, like the lost souls of the damned.

glass, a cracked clay pipe, and a towering stack of paper that leaned against a box-shaped contraption with brass hinges and a glass top . . .

Directly in front of me was the huge vat, set upon a tripod, its pungent contents bubbling furiously over a white-hot furnace. Thick clouds of crimson steam poured over the side of the cauldron and spilled out across the floor, writhing and squirming as they snaked towards me.

The toxic red steam coalesced and began to wind itself around my ankles, my calves, my knees. It burned my nostrils and stung my eyes. My head swam; my lungs were on fire. The heat made my skin prickle, and the noxious fumes left me gasping for breath as I fought desperately to free myself from the ropes that bound my hands and feet.

Just then, I felt a hand grasping my throat, pulling me out of the chair and forward onto my knees. A second hand grabbed the back of my head and thrust it forward until my face was inches above the bubbling liquid in the vat.

'Oh, how it burns, Barnaby Grimes,' the phantom's sinister voice hissed, before rising to a high-pitched crescendo. 'How it burns...'

CHAPTER
2

It was Ralph Booth-Prendegast, gentleman jockey and champion steeplechaser, who introduced me to Clarissa Oliphant. I'd helped him to solve the Hightown Derby doping scandal by catching the organ-grinder's monkey and its hypodermic needle, and 'Raffy' owed me a favour.

Clarissa Oliphant had been his governess when he was a lad and, when she came to him for help, Raffy passed the work my way. Of course, if I'd known then what I know now, I would have politely declined. Instead, that first meeting with Clarissa Oliphant proved to be the beginning of one of the strangest and darkest episodes of my life; one that, like the new fashion for photogravure portraiture that was starting to spread through the city, was to be etched indelibly into my memory.

It all started on one of those crisp autumn mornings, all too rare in the city, when the fallen leaves crunch underfoot, yellow and fringed with frost, and the sky is as blue as a morpho butterfly's wings – a Friday, as I recall. I highstacked across town, leaping from rooftop to gable, to the outskirts of Hightown.

I'm a tick-tock lad by trade, paid to deliver anything and everything anywhere in this great city of ours and as fast as I can because, tick-tock, time is money. For yours truly, that means climbing up the nearest drainpipe and running across the city's rooftops – or highstacking – as we tick-tock lads call it.

Taking care as I clambered over a jutting cornice, slippery with frost, I came down from the rooftops at the corner of Aspen Row. According to Raffy, Clarissa Oliphant, together with her brother Laurence, lived at number 12, and was expecting me.

The house was set in the middle of a terrace of smart town houses, with ornate black railings and white bow-windows. I climbed the marble steps, raised my swordstick and rapped smartly on the shiny black door.

Moments later, it was opened by a pretty parlourmaid, a strand of curly, blond hair escaping from her laced mobcap, and eyes of deep cornflower blue gazing directly into mine.

'Barnaby Grimes,' I announced with a smile, noticing the band of freckles that crossed the bridge of her dainty nose, 'to see Miss Oliphant. I believe she's expecting me . . .'

'Show him in, Tilly,' boomed a voice from down the hall behind the maid, who returned my smile shyly and beckoned me to follow her.

She showed me into a small drawing room, where I was confronted by a tall, imposing woman with small, twinkling eyes and steel-grey hair, pulled back in a tight bun. The tailored navy-blue jacket she was wearing, with its three rows of mother-of-pearl buttons down the front, gave her a somewhat military air, while the long crisply pleated black skirt lent her the appearance of a half-opened umbrella. On her feet was a pair of surprisingly elegant-looking dancing pumps of black patent leather.

She folded her arms across her ample bosom, so broad and level you could have rested a laden tea tray upon it, and tilted back her head. 'Take a seat, Mr Grimes,' she said. 'Raffy spoke very highly of you, though I must admit I was expecting someone a little older . . .'

I sat down in one of the two worn leather armchairs by the gently smouldering fire, while Clarissa Oliphant took the other. There were glazed porcelain dogs at either end of the mantelpiece, and a large, loudly ticking clock fashioned from ebony, copper and glass at its centre. It was five to ten, I noticed. I was early. Looking up, my gaze rested upon a magnificent sword, fixed to the wall. Clarissa followed my gaze.

'An original Dalmatian sabre,' she said, her deep voice as severe as the expression on her face. Her gaze rested briefly yet knowingly, I thought, on the swordstick attached to my belt. 'The finest fencing sword money can buy,' she added, 'and the tool of my former profession. Before I retired, Mr Grimes, I was a duelling governess.'

'A duelling governess,' I repeated, impressed.

I'd heard of these legendary Amazons, but hadn't actually met one before. A hundred years ago, they'd been all the rage, employed to settle the disputes of their charges, the pampered sons of the nobility, too young to fight duels themselves. These duelling governesses would defend the honour of

'An original Dalmatian sabre,' she said, her deep voice as severe as the expression on her face.

their charges while they were young, and include in their education the fine art of fencing, so that by the time the little darlings reached maturity, they were able to fight – and win – their own duels.

'Of course, we're a dying breed these days,' Clarissa Oliphant was saying. 'Now it's all Latin primers and horse riding for the sons of the privileged, and swordplay is something taken up by . . . others.'

Again, her gaze strayed to the swordstick at my side.

'What is it exactly that you require, Miss Oliphant?' I asked politely. Clearly the former duelling governess hadn't asked me to visit her to talk about swordplay.

The clock on the mantelpiece struck ten o'clock. Clarissa waited for the chimes to finish before replying.

'Each day at roughly this hour, my brother Laurence leaves the house,' she began, her booming voice now a conspiratorial whisper.

As if on cue, at that moment, there came a dull thud from above our heads, followed by the sound of footsteps. They crossed the room in one direction, hollow and heavy and making the floorboards creak, then doubled back on themselves.

'My brother, Mr Grimes, has become most secretive,' she told me. 'Secretive, one might say, to the point of paranoia. I have no idea where he goes or what he does when he gets there. All I do know' – she paused dramatically, her small eyes fixed on the ceiling above – 'is that whatever it is, it is beginning to have an alarming effect on his health, both mental and physical. Oh, he used to be such a wonderful person, Mr Grimes, carefree and open, always ready to confide in his older sister and listen to her advice. But then something changed him . . . Of course, though I have nothing concrete to go on, I do have my suspicions . . .'

'Suspicions?' I echoed.

'When Laurence came down from university, he had developed a fascination with the new art of, as he called it, "painting with light". It was a fascination encouraged by some of his tutors there,' she told me. 'He was mesmerized by the idea of using light to capture the image of a person or object, or a scene from life, and experimented with all kinds of materials on which to imprint such images – copper, paper, glass . . .'

I'd heard of such images, and the strange characters who sought fame and fortune trying to capture them, from my good friend, Professor Pinkerton-Barnes. They went by many different names, such as daguerreotypes, talbotypes, ambrotypes, autochromes and carbon prints, though the most common term was 'photograph', taken from the Greek words for 'light' and 'to draw', and coined by Sir Evelyn Henkel to describe the images he produced.

'Of course, the production of an image is

not the most difficult part of the process,' Clarissa Oliphant was saying. 'It is the permanent fixing of that image which remains the real challenge. After the debacle at the Konigsburg Exposition, where Horst Silberschilling's magnificent reproduction of the Kaiser's horse faded away in front of the assembled crowd ten minutes after its unveiling, many believed that it was impossible, and I hoped Laurence had given up his own experiments.'

She glanced down and plucked a piece of lint from the folds of her skirt, rubbed it between her forefinger and thumb and flicked it away. In the room above, the pacing abruptly ceased. Clarissa's brow furrowed.

'He certainly stopped talking about his "oliphantypes",' she said. 'But he gave up his position at the law practice and took to disappearing into the city every day and returning late at night,' she said, her deep voice faltering. 'And then there was that horrible accident . . .'

'Accident?' I said.

Clarissa grimaced. 'His face was badly burned down one side,' she said, the tips of her fingers trailing across her right cheek and round her jaw. 'Not that he'd tell me what had happened. Refused to even discuss it. He called for Tilly to fetch bandages and dressed the wound himself. The curious thing was,' she added thoughtfully, 'despite the obvious pain he was in, he seemed strangely excited, his eyes sparkling more brightly than I'd seen them in months.' She shook her head. 'That was three weeks ago, Mr Grimes, and frankly, I've had enough of his secrecy!'

Just then, the door in the room above us slammed shut. The next moment, the heavy footsteps were stomping down the stairs. Clarissa Oliphant was on her feet in an instant and marching towards the door.

'Keep your head down, Mr Grimes,' she hissed back at me. 'I don't want him to know you're here.'

I sank down in the chair. Clarissa opened the door and stepped into the hallway.

'Is that you, Laurence, dear?' she called, her voice booming up the stairwell. 'Where are you off to?'

'Out,' came a quiet, clipped reply.

I peered round the side of the chair and past Clarissa, who was standing in the doorway, her hands on her hips. A gaunt figure appeared on the stairs behind her. He was wearing a baggy overcoat of dark-green fustian weave, narrow breeches and heavy brown boots. Clasped in his right hand was a carved ebony cane. He seemed to be in a hurry.

He spun round the newel post at the bottom of the stairs and swept past his sister, his coat flapping. From what little I could see, he was a handsome man, with his sister's strong features, though his dark eyes had a haunted look to them and his cheeks were sallow and sunken-looking. I caught a glimpse of an angry red scar on the side of his face, visible despite the wide-brimmed Brompton pulled down low on his head.

The next moment, the front door slammed shut.

Clarissa Oliphant hurried back inside the drawing room, her face pinched and glowering.

'He's quite impossible!' she exclaimed, reaching into a pocket and taking out a crisp banknote. 'Follow him, Mr Grimes,' Clarissa ordered. 'I want to know where he goes and what he does, and when you have the information, return here to me and you shall have another one of these for your trouble.'

She pressed the note into my hand.

'Leave it to me, Miss Oliphant,' I said, jumping up from the chair and heading for the window. 'I'm on my way.'

CHAPTER
3

It felt good to be outside. Standing on the window-ledge at the back of the house, high above the small back garden below, I realized just how oppressive the atmosphere inside had been. Charged with suspicion and recriminations and matters that dare not be voiced, it had clung to me like a cold, rain-sodden blanket. Now, I had thrown it off, and I filled my lungs with the fresh, bright morning.

Behind me, the sash-window lowered with a rumble and a swoosh, and I turned to see Clarissa Oliphant looking back at me through the glass, her face grim. Despite Raffy's high opinion of his former governess, I hadn't warmed to her. She seemed rather overbearing and controlling, and for a moment I found myself sympathizing with her brother's attempts at privacy.

Then I felt the crisp banknote in the third pocket of my poacher's waistcoat and imagined a second one, just like it, nestling beside it. Clarissa Oliphant was a concerned sister, I told myself with a sly smile, worried about her younger brother's welfare . . .

Twisting round to face the wall, I swung my leg across to the adjacent drainpipe and shinned my way to the top as nimbly as a ferret up a trouser leg. I hauled myself over the jutting gutter, scurried up the firewall, arms outstretched for balance, and crossed over the ridge tiles. On the far side, I peered down into the street below.

Laurence Oliphant was already at the end of the row of houses, his wispy hair and dark-green coat flapping as he rounded the corner and strode off down the main street. He was walking so fast, I didn't dare let him out of my sight for a moment, and I knew I would have to use all my highstacking skills to keep up.

I followed him closely, deftly Tuppenny-Stepping my way along the terrace. Then, just before Aspen Row joined Fenugreek Road, I made use of some temporary scaffolding and a jutting buttress to cross the street.

I kept to the shadows wherever possible, my head down, so as not to be seen. Not that I thought Laurence Oliphant was about to notice me. Lost in his own thoughts, the man was marching along the pavement, his cane swinging as he cut a swathe through the other cobblestone-creepers. The local constabulary, on the other hand, was a different matter. The city police took a dim view of highstacking, and the last thing I wanted was to be apprehended by a red-faced plod threatening to throw the book at me.

I followed Oliphant as he turned right at

the old Navy Memorial, then right again where Cutpurse Walk crosses Broadacre. He was heading eastwards, away from well-to-do Hightown towards the altogether less salubrious East End district of Gastown.

There was no wind that day, not a breath. And as the industrial hub of the city came closer, the air grew thick and curdled with the acrid smoke and steam that billowed up from the glue factories and gasworks, forges, foundries and coal furnaces below.

Above my head, a vast swirling flock of starlings, gathering for their winter migration, flickered through the air. They darkened the sun and filled the sky with their metallic cries. For an instant I joined them, flying through the air from a soot-encrusted cornice to the flat roof of a brick warehouse in a classic Peabody Roll.

Jumping to my feet, I glanced down at the street below and saw Laurence Oliphant striding down the crowded street. Then, as I watched, I was horrified to see him do the most extraordinary thing.

Head down and shoulders hunched, he shot out the hand clutching the cane and tripped a passer-by, an elderly gentleman in a grubby overcoat, who toppled into the street and straight into the path of an oncoming coal merchant's dray. The driver of the dray tugged hard on the reins. The dray swerved to avoid the gentleman and collided with a cart laden with barrels of apples, leaving both vehicles on their sides.

Still in harness, the felled horses whinnied with terror, their eyes rolling and hooves kicking uselessly at the air. Sacks and barrels had spilled their contents. The driver of the dray lay on the road, blood pouring from his head. Crowds swarmed round the accident, some stopping to help out, others seizing the opportunity to stuff their bags, pockets and aprons with free coal.

Laurence Oliphant continued through the

gathering mayhem, his cane swinging like a constable's truncheon, clearing a path before him. He paused once, looking behind him, and I thought for an instant he might have been regretting his action. But he merely stooped down and retrieved a bright-red apple from the pavement, which he rubbed on the lapel of his fustian overcoat and bit into as he continued on his way.

I followed him, leaving the chaotic scene behind, feeling sick to my stomach with what I'd just witnessed. I was beginning to suspect that Clarissa Oliphant's fears for her brother's mental state were well-founded. As we went deeper into Gastown, the buildings became increasingly rundown and ramshackle, with cramped living quarters built on top of dark sweatshops and filthy workhouses. I had to take care not to miss my footing on the cracked roof tiles and crumbling brickwork. At the end of Blue Boar Lane, Oliphant turned abruptly onto a narrow alleyway, and stopped in front of the battered, padlocked door of a squat building halfway along. He rummaged in the pockets of his breeches for a key.

Blood Alley. Of all places!

Of course, I knew Blood Alley by reputation. The place was notorious. It lay at the centre of Gastown, the dark heart of the grimy district. Of course, there are other seedy parts of the city, each with their own problems, from the grinding poverty of the Rats Nest to the brutal gang violence of Gatling Quays. But Gastown was different. It was a sinister, brooding place, full of shuttered workshops and ominously boarded up buildings, behind whose facades all manner of disreputable enterprises were rumoured to take place. And of all the tightly packed streets, Blood Alley's reputation was indisputably the worst.

Apparently, years earlier, tanneries had lined the alley on both sides, the red dyes and acid chemicals of the so-called 'odiferous trade' sluicing down the gutters like blood. It was this foul effluence that gave the alley its name. These days, the tanneries, along with their foul vats filled with stale urine and stinking dung, were gone. The buildings had been turned into two rows of industrial lock-ups, bolted and shuttered against prying eyes.

The infamous Gutrot Gang were rumoured to produce the foulest, most intoxicating stevedore brandy in Blood Alley, while it was said that the Mog Shavers, the largest gang of cat-skinners in the city, manufactured their 'ermine' fur coats here too. Counterfeiters, document forgers, scammers, skimmers and hot-toddy merchants lurked behind every locked door, each one a fortress against the raids of the city constabulary, which were few and far between.

Laurence Oliphant disappeared hurriedly inside the building and pulled the door shut behind him. I heard bolts slamming into place. There was a small window next to the door, but as I lowered myself onto a wedge-shaped roof opposite, I saw that, unsurprisingly, it had been boarded up. I shinned down a rusting drainpipe and landed lightly on the cobbles. In front of me, to the right of the lock-up, was a dank ginnel, which took me to the back of the row. Each of the lock-ups had its own high-walled back yard, screening them from view.

Carefully, I eased myself up the wall, my fingertips and points of my boots finding purchase in the crumbling mortar between the brickwork. It was slow work, but after a couple of minutes I was able to peer over the shards of broken glass that crenellated the top of the eight-foot wall.

I glimpsed an untidy yard, strewn with dented zinc tanks and twists of greening copper. There was a window to the right of the back door, glazed rather than boarded. Taking care to avoid the razor-sharp glass, I was attempting to get a better view when all at once there was a bloodcurdling roar, and in a blurred rush of glistening slaver and glinting teeth, a monstrous hound reared up at me and thrust its snarling mouth toward my face.

I recoiled, almost losing my grip on the wall, my heart hammering with fright. The creature dropped back down out of sight, only to reappear a moment later as it lunged up at me.

Transfixed, I stared at the hideous beast, my legs trembling. Up on its hind legs it must have been six feet tall at least. It was lean and muscular, and its rough, matted fur bristled as it jumped repeatedly at the top of the wall, only to fall back again. It eyed me furiously from beneath bushy wire-like eyebrows, its eyeballs rolling in their sockets. Frothing drool dripped from yellow fangs as its scarred jaws opened, and a low, menacing growl emerged from the back of its throat. I knew that it would have liked nothing better than to tear me limb from limb.

I'd been stupid. Careless. Most of these

. . . a monstrous hound reared up at me and thrust its snarling mouth toward my face.

lock-ups were likely to be guarded by savage dogs, and I should have known that Laurence Oliphant would want to protect his own secrets from prying eyes. As if to confirm my thoughts, the yards along the alley erupted in a cacophony of angry barks and howling as the chained beasts within them joined the chorus.

From inside the lock-up, there came the sound of a door slamming. I let go of the wall and dropped to the cobbles below, hitting the ground running – but not before I saw the face at the window.

It was scarcely human. One disembodied eye, grinning teeth, wisps of hair and patches of skin, all disconnected, as if half the face had been ripped away. But worse, far worse, I realized as I ran back down Blood Alley and round the corner, was not that I had seen this hideous creature, but that it had clearly seen me.

CHAPTER
4

$\mathscr{I}$ sat myself down on the flat roof of a
six-storey brown brick tenement block
on Prospect Avenue, where Gastown borders
the more upmarket Bishopsgate, my legs
dangling over the side. I was still shaken up
by the events in Blood Alley, and had decided
to take a moment to collect my thoughts
before I continued back to Clarissa Oliphant's
house.

I'd been confronted by watchdogs before
of course. It came with my line of work.
Scruffy mutts and mongrels for the most
part, ill-fed and bad-tempered. But the dog
I'd encountered in Blood Alley was not one

of these. I'd recognized it as a pedigree Moravian boarhound, a noble breed usually associated with country estates rather than Gastown lock-ups. Good-natured and loyal as a rule, this one must have been brutally treated to turn it into the vicious beast I'd encountered.

Had Laurence Oliphant done this? I wondered. Or did the creature belong to the hideous apparition I'd glimpsed at the window? And if so, then who was that foul, deformed monster? Questions were buzzing around my head, when all at once I heard the sound of desperate wailing . . .

I looked round and noticed a cat on the adjacent fire escape. It was clinging hold of a cast-iron rung, its ears pinned back and body trembling, caterwauling for help. I guessed that it had been running from the unwanted attentions of a watchdog when it had taken to the stairs of the fire escape, leaping up the cast-iron rungs to safety – until its confidence had run out, that is. Now it was stuck, unable to return the way it had come and incapable of making that final leap onto the roof; a manoeuvre that any self-respecting tomcat would have managed without a second thought.

But this was no alley-cat, no ratter, no sleek pigeon hunter or backstreet mog. No, the quivering specimen before me was clearly a lap-cat. A Persepolis blue, if I was not mistaken; a plump and pampered household pet, and with a pedigree every bit as impressive as the Moravian boarhound's.

The cat's wailing hit an agonized crescendo. It stared at me pitifully, as if pleading for my help. I didn't have the heart to ignore it.

'All right, you win,' I told it, as I headed back along the roof. 'I'm coming.'

This was easier said than done, as I soon discovered. Though petrified of the yawning drop below, the cat seemed even more terrified of yours truly. As I lowered myself onto the first of the diagonal iron stairs of the fire escape, the stupid creature yowled and shrank back. I stopped at once and leaned down.

'Shhh,' I whispered. 'It's all right. I'm not going to hurt you . . .'

The cat trembled. I took another step, trying hard not to make the metal stairs vibrate. It let out a cry of terror and scrabbled back awkwardly along the rusted rung.

'It's all right,' I repeated, stopping a second time. 'Just stay where you are. There's a good cat.'

But the cat remained unsure. Claws out and fur on end, it went rigid as I got closer. I paused on the rung just above it, twisted round so my back was to the ladder, and looked down. The creature stared back, bared its teeth and hissed. I crouched and, whispering reassurances, reached towards it, ready to scoop it up.

All at once, with a terrified screech, the cat lashed out, its claws slashing at my outstretched fingers. I withdrew my hand just in time and straightened up, ripping the front of my poacher's waistcoat on a jutting bolt as I did so. I heard something hard clatter down the metal flights of stairs below me, and saw half a dozen business cards flutter away . . .

The cat squirmed round, braced itself and took a flying leap off the edge of the ladder and onto the adjacent window-ledge. I glared at it furiously, and had half a mind to leave the ridiculous creature where it was. But then it mewled piteously, staring at me with those wide panic-stricken eyes.

Taking a deep breath, I lowered myself to the rung below and edged closer to the window-ledge. The cat eyed me suspiciously, its fur on end.

'I'm going to rescue you, whether you like it or not,' I told it.

Gripping the side of the stairs with my left hand, I pulled my coalstack hat from my head with my right. I stared ahead, calculating the

'I'm going to rescue you, whether you like it or not,' I told it.

angles, and counted down from five. When I hit zero, I tightened my grip on the stair rail and swung out into mid air. As I drew level with the window-ledge, I brought my hat down over the cat and dragged it towards me. Then, just as it reached the edge of the sill, I twisted my wrist, flipping the hat round so that the cat dropped down inside it, and swung back to the fire escape.

It had worked like a dream. As for the cat, it offered no further resistance, instead lying still in the darkness at the bottom of my coalstack hat. I tucked the hat under my arm and descended the fire escape, planning to release the cat when I reached the bottom.

That was when I discovered I'd had an audience. I heard the sound of clapping hands and an excited voice calling out from below.

'Bobbin! Bobbin!' the voice cried, and I looked down to see a slim, even-featured woman staring up at me, her blue eyes radiant with happiness and relief.

I jumped down beside her and proffered my hat. 'This cat is yours, I take it.'

The woman reached inside, pulled the cat out and dangled it before her. It went limp and purred loudly.

'Bobbin, you naughty cat,' she said, shaking her head in mock anger. She tucked him inside her shawl. 'He's mine, all right,' she told me, smiling brightly as I replaced my hat on my head. 'Thank you so much for rescuing him, Mr . . . ?'

'Barnaby Grimes, tick-tock lad,' I told her, smiling back. 'Glad to be of assistance.'

The woman frowned. 'But your waistcoat,' she said, her face creasing with concern. 'It's completely ruined.'

I looked down. The bolt I'd snagged my waistcoat on had caused considerable damage. Three of the pockets were hanging by a thread, while a fourth was missing completely, and there was a gaping hole down the right-hand seam.

'It is a bit of a mess,' I conceded. 'I'll have to take it to the tailor to be repaired . . .'

'I wouldn't hear of it,' she said, and seized me by the sleeve. 'One good turn deserves another.'

Taking me by the arm, she led me along the sidewalk, talking nineteen to the dozen as we went. Her name, she told me, was Mrs Clare Gosney, and she was a bespoke seamstress by profession. She ran a little shop with her daughter, Molly, and her beloved Bobbin was, as I'd thought, a Persepolis blue, and rather valuable into the bargain.

'Though absolutely priceless to me,' she added, and hugged the purring bundle wrapped up in her shawl.

We came to a small shop at the end of the street, its front window overflowing with rolls of lace, bolts of material and an assortment of wooden tailors' dummies, the finely cut clothes they were modelling somewhat spoiled by the way they leaned drunkenly against one another. Above the door was a sign, painted in elegant serif lettering. *Gosney and Daughter : Fine Millinery and Dressmaking.*

'Here we are,' she announced.

A doorbell jangled as she shouldered her way inside. I followed her and found myself in a small room, made smaller by the number of tailors' dummies and bundles of cloth which filled every available inch of space. There was an oak counter directly in front of me, piled high with folded items of clothing, each one with a card of neatly written instructions pinned to it. A black leather-bound book lay beside them. Behind the counter were three tables. Two of them were laid out with pieces of crimson material, white chalk marking the places from which collars, sleeves and sides would be cut out. At the third table sat a girl, fourteen or fifteen years old, with a long braided pigtail and the brownest eyes I had ever seen.

She put down her needlework and leaped from her stool. 'You *found* her!' she exclaimed.

'Not me, Molly,' said Mrs Gosney. She hung her shawl on a hook behind the door. 'It was Barnaby here. Mr Barnaby Grimes, a tick-tock lad. He rescued Bobbin from the top of a fire escape, didn't he, Bobbin?' she said, and pressed her nose into the cat's face. 'And he ruined his poacher's waistcoat in the process.'

She placed Bobbin down. The cat trotted over to the glowing coal fire on the far side of the room, and curled up on the rug in front of it. Mrs Gosney watched him indulgently for a moment, a smile on her lips, then turned to her daughter.

'So I'm going to make him a brand-new one,' she announced.

'Really,' I said, 'there's no need to—'

But she silenced me, pressing the tip of her finger to her lips. She pulled a cloth tape measure from around her neck and turned to me.

'Take off your jacket.'

I did as I was told and she took my measurements, one by one. Under my arms, across my shoulders and around my waist, noting everything down in the black leather book. Then, stepping back, she looked me carefully up and down, and made a charcoal sketch of the waistcoat's design, noting every pocket, every loop and clasp, every button, toggle and hook.

'There,' she said at last. 'Leave your old waistcoat with me. If you come back in a few days, I'll have the new one ready for you—'

Her words were abruptly drowned out by something clattering noisily down the cobblestones outside. I poked my head out of the open door, only to jump back again as a familiar figure sped past in a blur, skidded wildly and crashed headlong into the lamppost on the corner.

I hurried over to the stricken figure, Mrs Gosney and her daughter close on my heels.

'Will?' I said softly. 'Will Farmer!'

At the sound of my voice, Will Farmer's eyes snapped open. He sat bolt upright.

'Barnaby!' he said, and grinned. 'What do you think of my new invention?'

CHAPTER 5

I helped my good friend, Will Farmer, to his feet and he dusted himself down, seemingly none the worse for wear. Will was a tick-tock lad just like yours truly, and had rooms next to mine on Caged Lark Lane.

'Well?' he said. 'What do you think, Barnaby?'

He pointed to the object lying in the gutter. I'd never seen anything like it before. It consisted of a bevelled board about a yard long and a foot wide, with four spoked wheels that had been attached to the underside with two stout brass axles.

'This,' said Will proudly, 'is a little

something I've been working on.' He flipped the board over with his boot and stamped down on one end, sending the contraption leaping into the air. He caught it with one hand. 'I call it a wheelboard.'

'A wheelboard?' I repeated.

'I made it myself,' he said, nodding. 'Out of a piano lid and four perambulator wheels. Gaffer Jones, that ironmonger down Solder Lane, made up the axles for me to my own design. It's brilliant for getting around town. I got the idea when I saw a piano fall off a delivery cart at the top of Coppervane Hill last week and roll all the way down to Goose-fair Square.'

'So this is all your own work,' I said, impressed.

It looked intriguing, and was far less cumbersome than a horse and carriage, though clearly far trickier to bring to a halt.

'I'm still getting the hang of it,' added Will, 'but it's really good fun. And given time,

Barnaby, I believe wheelboarding could become all the rage!'

Will stopped and his mouth flopped open like a pond carp on a paving stone. I followed his gaze. He was staring at Molly Gosney, who stared back, her face flushed.

'Will Farmer,' I said. 'Allow me to introduce Mrs Clare Gosney and her daughter, Molly.'

'P-p-pleased t-to meet you,' stuttered Will.

'Come, Molly,' said Mrs Gosney, smiling and giving me a wink. 'We've got a waistcoat to make. Mr Grimes, Mr Farmer, good day to you both.'

They turned and started walking away.

'Will,' I told him, 'I've got to be going. I'll see you back at Caged Lark Lane.'

'Uh-huh,' he muttered, but I knew he hadn't heard a word. He had ears and eyes for Molly Gosney alone. I waited. But it was only when the bell above the shop door jangled softly and the object of his attention followed her mother inside that Will looked round. 'You said something, Barnaby?'

I laughed and bade him goodbye a second time, and we went our separate ways. Will clattered off down the hill on his wheelboard, while I returned to the fire escape on Prospect Avenue. I noticed a couple of the business cards I'd dropped lying on the pavement, together with a small leatherbound notebook which my friend, Professor Pinkerton-Barnes, had given me to aid my research into one of his hare-brained theories.

The professor – or PB, as he liked his friends to call him – had all sort of theories on animal behaviour, everything from bipedal voles to choral-singing crows. Recently, he'd theorized that sparrow hawks were abandoning their farmland habitat and venturing into the city to prey off the vermin that lived there. He'd asked me to keep a running tally of any nesting sites I saw at the top of the tallest buildings while highstacking, so that he could compile comprehensive tables. I'd had the notebook for more than a month, jotting down the size and location of each one I spotted. And I'd spotted quite a lot. As to how many exactly, I wasn't sure, but the notebook was practically full.

I pulled my fob-watch from my coat pocket and checked the time. It was a quarter past one. I had to return to Clarissa Oliphant's house in Hightown, but since I was quite close to the professor's university rooms, I decided to drop in on him first. Quite apart from anything else, it had been a long and tiring morning, and I was in need of a cup of PB's excellent Assam Black tea.

I arrived on the roof of the imposing white-stone academy minutes later and shinned down a drainpipe to the window sill of the professor's laboratory. Peering through the grimy glass, I saw PB stooped over a workbench, his back towards me. I tapped on the window, and he turned. I don't know who was more surprised; PB to see me crouching there on his window sill, or yours truly to see his swaddled head.

'Barnaby,' he said, striding to the window and opening it.

'PB,' I said, grinning as I jumped inside. 'What's with the new bonnet?'

The professor grimaced. 'Toothache, Barnaby,' he said. 'A rather tiresome case of toothache.' Despite the bandage, which he'd wrapped over his ears, round his chin and secured at the top of his head with a floppy bow, I could see that the left side of his jaw was badly swollen.

He returned to the workbench behind him. A cluster of open bottles stood at its centre, a pipette lying in front of them and a test tube in a retort standing to their right.

'I was just preparing a little something,' he explained, 'to ease the pain.'

I sniffed the air. 'Cloves,' I said.

'Oil of cloves, indeed,' he said. 'Among other things. Tincture of iodine, camomile and lavender. Anise ... And a splash of laudanum,' he added.

I peered over his shoulder as he continued working, counting off the drops of the various liquids and shaking them together. He was clearly in a lot of pain, his face grimacing with every movement he made.

'Let me, PB,' I told him, taking the pipette from his shaking hand. 'Now, how many drops of this exactly?'

'Twelve,' he said miserably. 'Though I doubt it'll help. It's the third batch I've made in as many days, and the pain's as bad as ever.'

I nodded thoughtfully.

'I've got an idea, something I came across in Dalhousie's *Handbook of Dentistry* the other day,' I said, turning to him. 'I'll need a small piece of zinc and a stout pair of scissors.'

Wincing with pain, the professor waved a

hand at the drawer. 'You'll find everything you need in there,' he said, and added wearily, 'I'm going to sit down for a moment.'

The professor was always fashioning curious contraptions to do with his experiments, and the drawer was stuffed full of various leftover bits and pieces. There were lengths of wire, cogs and chains, rubber tubing, and a vast assortment of nuts, bolts and washers . . .

'This is zinc, isn't it?' I said, waving a small, irregular-shaped sheet of mottled metal in front of him.

He was sitting with one hand pressed gingerly to his swollen jaw. He opened his eyes.

'Zinc?' he said. 'Yes, it is, but . . .'

'All in good time,' I told him.

I seized a pair of scissors from the drawer and, holding up the zinc plate, carefully cut out a small circle about the same size as a thruppenny piece. I could feel PB's gaze resting on me as I did so, intrigued, despite the pain of his toothache. I fished in my breeches pocket for a silver tanner.

'Here,' I said, placing both the small coin and the smaller disc of zinc in PB's outstretched hand. 'Put the two pieces of metal together, and clamp the pair of them next to your bad tooth.'

The professor looked perplexed, but did as he was told. He closed his eyes. A minute later, he opened them again.

'Ip's pingling,' he muttered.

'Tingling?' I said. 'It's supposed to. Wait a bit longer.'

While PB sat there, the two discs of metal clamped between his jaws, I crossed the laboratory and put a kettle on the stove. I was looking forward to a nice cup of Assam Black more than ever. I was warming the pot when I realized that the professor was standing behind me. I turned to see him grinning broadly.

'Quite remarkable!' he exclaimed. He was holding the two pieces of metal in one hand, and the bandage in his other. 'The pain has gone!'

I smiled, pleased that my little experiment had worked so well.

'The zinc and silver acted together with your saliva as a galvanic battery. It produced an electric current that worked on the nerves of the tooth, and relieved the pain,' I told PB proudly. 'Dalhousie has made some real breakthroughs in the field.'

'You and your fields of interest never fail to amaze me, Barnaby,' said PB approvingly. He took over the tea-making duties, swilling the hot water away and adding tea leaves to the pot. 'I never know what you're going to come up with next.'

'Funny you should say that, PB,' I replied, 'because just recently I've become interested in the science of photogravure.'

'Is that so?' said PB. He chuckled as he

poured us each a cup of steaming tea. 'I have to say that, for me, it is the photographic capture of movement that fascinates me most. It would help so much with my work to be able to analyse the gallop of a horse or the wingbeat of a bird . . .'

'Talking of birds,' I said, as I remembered the reason for my visit, 'I dropped by to return your notebook, PB. It's full . . .'

'Excellent work, Barnaby,' he said. He looked up and smiled, his tongs poised over the sugar bowl. 'Now, is it one lump or two?' he asked. 'I always forget.'

'No sugar for me,' I reminded him, then stifled a smile as the professor proceeded to put six sugar lumps into his own small cup. He passed me my tea, ushered me across to the wing-back chair at the end of the room and perched himself on the edge of the ottoman opposite.

'Photogravure,' he said thoughtfully. 'Or photography, as I prefer to call it.' He stirred his tea. 'I knew one of its earliest exponents, Dean Henry Dodson. We were up at university together, with adjacent rooms in New College, though he was several years older than me and already writing his doctorate.'

I took a sip of tea, the aromatic liquid bursting with flavour on my tongue. No one, but no one, made tea like Professor Pinkerton-Barnes.

'A strange fellow, something of a maverick,' he was saying, 'and, just like you, Barnaby, he had an interest in a vast range of subjects.' He frowned. 'Everything from medieval alchemy to ancient pagan cults, from mechanical calculating machines to apparatus designed to manipulate light . . .'

'And he invented photography?' I asked.

'Invented,' the professor repeated softly, and took a sip of his own tea. 'From my experience, Barnaby, such things are rarely the invention of a single person.' He smiled.

'Rather they grow from the accumulated work of many minds all seeking universal truths.' PB shook his head ruefully. 'Though there are always squabbles breaking out between rival scientists as to who thought of what first,' he added. He took another sip of tea. 'But yes, Barnaby, Dean Henry Dodson is certainly a pioneer of the exciting new science, or art, of painting with light. And fascinating stuff it is, too . . .'

As so often happened when the professor and I got talking over a pot of Assam Black, we became so immersed in our conversation that we both lost all track of time. Before I knew it, night had fallen and the lamplighters had come and gone. I heard the bells of Montgomery Hall chiming. It was seven o'clock and, as I noted the lateness of the hour, Clarissa Oliphant's disapproving face suddenly appeared before me. I placed my cup and saucer hurriedly on the table and jumped to my feet.

'I must go, Professor,' I said. 'I'm late. Thank you for my tea.'

'And thank you, Barnaby, for your cure,' he replied. 'I don't know what I'd have done without you.'

The evening rush, when crowds of cobble-stone-creepers compete with countless horse and carriages in the city streets below, was all but over as I highstacked back across town. The air was still, the sky clear and, with the temperature dropping fast, I had to be careful not to slip on the roof tiles as a thick hoar-frost formed. Three quarters of an hour later, a perfectly executed Drainpipe Sluice brought me down in front of 12 Aspen Row. It was a little late for the genteel folk of Hightown to be receiving unannounced visitors, but I guessed that for me, Clarissa Oliphant would make an exception.

I was right.

'Mr Grimes!' she exclaimed enthusiastically when Tilly the pretty maid showed me into the drawing room. 'Tell me what you have been able to discover.'

Seated before a roaring fire, I told her everything I'd found out that day. Everything, that is, except for my outlandish thoughts about the ghastly apparition that had stared out at me from the window which, in the clear light of day, seemed too fantastical to put into words.

'I glimpsed a figure at the window,' I told her simply. 'A strange figure that I don't think was your brother, Miss Oliphant, though I couldn't be absolutely sure . . .'

'A strange figure!' exclaimed Clarissa Oliphant, then paused, for at that moment the door opened and in strode her brother, Laurence Oliphant. The collar of his baggy green overcoat was up, the wide brim of his Brompton down, while a thick, tartan scarf covered his mouth and nose. He glanced across at me, and in that fleeting moment, I saw a flicker of recognition in his eyes.

He glanced across at me, and in that fleeting moment, I saw a flicker of recognition in his eyes.

'Clarissa, I think you owe me an explanation,' he said, turning to his sister.

'Indeed,' said Clarissa. 'Mr Grimes was just leaving.'

She ushered me to the door, pressed that second crisp banknote into my hand with a soft 'thank you', and closed the door behind me. I was glad to be out of the room, I can tell you. There had been a look of despair in Clarissa's Oliphant's eyes and, for a moment, I felt guilty about my original thoughts that she was overbearing and controlling. This was a proud and concerned sister, at the end of her tether. What was more, despite the heat from the fire, the look that Laurence Oliphant had given me had chilled me to the marrow in my bones. I was heading for the front door, when Tilly the maid came out of the scullery and took me by the arm.

'Oh, Barnaby!' she exclaimed, her pretty eyes clouded with concern. 'They're going to have one of those rows of theirs. And

I hate it when they argue, I really hate it!'

In the drawing room, I could hear Laurence's voice, shrill and peevish, growing increasingly agitated, and Clarissa, speaking firmly, endeavouring to calm him down. It wasn't having the desired effect.

'Stop trying to control me!' Laurence protested.

'But, Laurence, dear . . .'

'Snooping round and prying into my affairs. It's intolerable.'

'But I worry so for your well-being,' said Clarissa. 'You don't look after yourself, and you never had the strongest of constitutions, even as a boy. I'm concerned you're making yourself ill.'

'Well, don't be,' he snapped. 'I'm fine. And anyway, you're my sister, not my governess, and I'm not one of your precious pampered charges. Do you understand, Clarissa? I don't want your concern.'

'But my dear Laurence,' boomed Clarissa,

'all I want – all I have ever wanted – is what's best for you.'

'Then give me the money I need,' he shouted. 'I've made a great breakthrough, Clarissa, and I need funds to exploit its full potential. You have that strongbox full of gold sovereigns that Lord Riverhythe bequeathed you, which you hoard like a miser, while I, your own flesh and blood, have to beg and borrow to fund my work . . .'

'But what *is* this work, Laurence?' Clarissa asked, beseechingly. 'You won't talk of it. It's making you ill, and yet you ask me to invest my nest egg in it . . .'

'Well, if you won't cough up the gold,' screamed Laurence Oliphant, 'I'll take something I can sell, at least!'

'No, Laurence!' Clarissa Oliphant exclaimed, the motherly tone to her voice replaced by fierce emotion. 'Not that! You know how much it means to me.'

'And you know how much my work means

to me,' he shouted. 'I'm going to my studio. Do not attempt to follow me!'

The drawing-room door flew open and he stormed past Tilly and me in a blur of movement, his fustian weave overcoat flapping behind him.

'Laurence, dear,' Clarissa called after him. '*Laurence!*'

The front door slammed shut. Tilly and I exchanged glances. The next moment, Clarissa Oliphant appeared in the hallway.

'Bring me my smelling salts, Tilly,' she said wearily, 'I'm feeling a little faint.' She turned to me. 'Mr Grimes,' she said, a single eyebrow arched. 'You're still here, I see.'

I nodded as Tilly hurried off to the scullery, drying her eyes on her apron.

'My nerves,' she said, pushing behind her ear a strand of hair that had come loose from her bun. 'I don't know how much more of this I can take.'

'If there's anything I can do?' I told her.

She nodded, and I saw the resolve in her pursed lips. 'There is, Mr Grimes,' she said, her voice booming once more. 'Tomorrow morning, first thing, I want you to take me to this lock-up of Laurence's. I intend to have it out with him. It's time to put a stop to this nonsense once and for all.'

CHAPTER 6

First thing, she'd said, and first thing, I was there, knocking at 12 Aspen Row at eight o'clock on the dot. The door flew open and Clarissa Oliphant stood before me, dressed for the cold in a heavy calf-length greatcoat and an oversized green tam-o'-shanter. Her face was drawn and there were bags under her eyes. It didn't look as though she'd got a moment's sleep all night. She twirled an umbrella in her hand and thrust it forward.

'Lead on, Mr Grimes.'

We must have made an odd couple as we strode through town. Clarissa Oliphant, tall, portly and silver-haired, striding impatiently behind me as I led the way, anxious not to be trampled underfoot.

The city was busy. It was Saturday, and several streets and squares were lined with bustling market stalls. We picked our way through the crowds on Fenugreek Street and Marston Lane as I retraced the route I'd taken the previous day. There was a distinguished-looking gentleman in front of the old Navy Memorial, exchanging lapel pins for donations to the Old Sailors' Benevolent Fund. I paused to give him some spare change, causing Clarissa Oliphant to barrel into me and almost lose her footing on the cobbles.

'Come, Mr Grimes,' she insisted as I grabbed her elbow to steady her. 'There is no time for delay!'

Broadacre was thronging and, not for the first time, I looked up longingly at the rooftops overhead, wishing that I was up there, far above the heaving cobbled streets. Using her umbrella like a weapon, Clarissa drove forward, her top lip curling as the foul stench that hung permanently over Gastown grew stronger. She pulled a lace-edged handkerchief from her pocket and held it to her nose.

'Not far now,' I told her. We were on Blue Boar Lane. 'It's the next turning on the right.'

As we rounded the corner, I halted in my tracks. Something was not right.

The day before, Blood Alley had been deserted. Now there was a large group clustered around one of the lock-ups, staring intently and whispering to one another in hushed, urgent voices behind their hands. I noticed the 'Black Margery', a two-horse police carriage, parked at the end of the alley. A rotund constable, his face red and helmet askew, was guarding the open door of the lock-up, while from the back yards, every dog in the alley was furiously barking.

'Which one is Laurence's?' asked Clarissa

Oliphant purposefully, looking up and down
Blood Alley.

My stomach turned somersaults. 'That
one.' I pointed to the lock-up which was
attracting all the attention.

Clarissa Oliphant let out a little cry of
dismay. 'I knew something was wrong,' she
boomed.

She broke into an ungainly lolloping run,
her patent-leather pumps skidding on the
frosty cobbles. She pushed her way through
the gawping onlookers; I followed in her wake.
The constable stepped forward to bar her way,
but the indomitable governess brushed him
aside with her rolled umbrella, as though
parrying a blow from a fencing opponent.

'I'm Clarissa Oliphant,' she proclaimed as
she marched inside, 'sister of the owner of
this lock-up.'

I followed her. The constable protested.

'Oi, you can't go barging your way in 'ere!
This is a murder scene . . .'

The lock-up, I discovered, housed a laboratory studio. It was cramped and hot, and bathed in a blood-red light cast by the ornate brass gas lamp on the side wall, which had a length of crimson silk wrapped round its glass cowl. Planks of wood had been nailed across the windows, cutting out every scrap of daylight. It was like stepping into an infernal pit.

There was a bench to my left, with a sink and zinc trays set along it, and overladen shelves above. To my right were cupboards, and a table bowing under the weight of the equipment piled upon it, while around my head, pegged to a clothes line that spanned the air and fluttering as I walked past, were numerous squares of paper. Each one was an oliphantype, the images of the faces that Laurence Oliphant had captured staring back at me impassively.

At the far end of the room, I saw a stout figure in a hound's-tooth mackintosh crouched down beside an upturned cauldron. As Clarissa and I approached, he looked round, his face flushed in the red glow. He was jowly, with a hooked nose and dark, deep-set eyes, and was clasping a large magnifying glass in his right hand. On his head was a polished tub-belly bowler of charcoal grey, the latest fashion for detectives in the city constabulary. He looked the pair of us up and down, stroked his moustache then climbed slowly to his feet.

'I,' he said officiously, 'am Inspector Clackett. And who might you be?'

'I'm Barnaby Grimes,' I told him. 'Tick-tock lad. And this is Clarissa Oliphant, sister of . . .'

I fell silent. As the inspector had stood up, a body, lying in the flickering shadows at the base of the pot-bellied vat, revealed itself. Clarissa Oliphant gasped and clamped the lace handkerchief to her mouth. I struggled not to gag at the gruesome sight before me.

The face of the body lying there was unrecognizable. Barely human in appearance, the entire head had been burned by the corrosive contents of the up-turned cauldron – skin, hair and features melted like candle wax.

And deeply embedded in the corpse's chest was Clarissa Oliphant's duelling sword, its jewelled hilt gleaming like beads of blood.

'Laurence,' I heard Clarissa whisper, and she rushed forward, her arms outstretched.

The inspector seized her by the wrist. 'Do not touch the body, Miss Oliphant,' he cautioned. 'It has been doused in something highly caustic.'

Clarissa visibly shrank. 'But what . . . what has happened, Inspector?'

'That,' he told her grimly, 'is what I am attempting to establish. It appears that the victim was stabbed through the heart, and that the murderer subsequently attempted to dispose of the body by dissolving it in chemicals. I put the time of death somewhere between midnight and four in the morning, a time that coincides with witness reports of a loud and violent disturbance.' His eyes narrowed. 'Can you confirm that this is your brother, Laurence Oliphant?'

'They're his . . . his clothes,' Clarissa replied weakly. 'I bought him that overcoat myself. Fustian weave,' she said, 'the best that money could buy. He always had such a delicate chest . . .' Her eyes filled with tears as she realized what she'd said.

All three of us stared at the sword sticking out of the victim's chest. From the back yard, the sound of furious barking became louder, more insistent. Inspector Clackett took a sharp intake of breath.

'Can you shed any light on the murder weapon?' he asked.

Clarissa nodded miserably. 'It belongs to me,' she said, a fact that seemed to turn the air brittle.

The inspector's beady eyes narrowed.

'I was a duelling governess by profession,' she explained, 'and that was a sword presented to me by Lord Riverhythe when I left his service. It's a Dalmatian sabre,' she added. 'Extremely valuable . . .'

'And can you explain how your Dalmatian sabre came to be here, Miss Oliphant?'

'I . . . that is,' she faltered. 'Laurence . . . I had it displayed above my drawing-room mantelpiece, and last night Laurence took it. I believed he intended to sell it.'

'And at what time exactly did this occur?' the inspector asked, pulling a notebook from the top pocket of his jacket and licking his pencil.

Clarissa frowned. 'Eight. Eight fifteen, wasn't it, Barnaby?'

The inspector turned to me. 'You witnessed this?'

'I was at the Oliphants' house yesterday evening,' I told him. 'I can confirm everything that Miss Oliphant has told you.'

'You saw Laurence Oliphant leave with the sword?' the inspector queried, his dark eyes boring into mine.

The barking grew louder, and was punctuated with angry shouts and curses from what I supposed were exasperated constables.

I shook my head. 'I was in the hallway,' I told him. 'But I *heard* the altercation between Miss Oliphant and her brother,' I said, 'after which he stormed past me and left the house.'

'Did you actually see him with the sword in question?' the inspector persisted.

I had to admit I hadn't. 'It all happened so fast,' I told him.

The inspector turned his attention back to Clarissa Oliphant. 'Where were you between the hours of midnight and four o'clock this morning?' he demanded.

'I . . . I . . .' She looked startled. 'In my bed, Inspector,' she said.

'In your bed,' the inspector said slowly,

making a careful note in his notebook. 'So you have no alibi.' He took a deep breath, his eyes narrowing. 'If you would accompany me to the station, Miss Oliphant, there are a few facts I would like to get straight.'

I expected Clarissa to object, but the fight seemed to have gone out of her. She nodded weakly and hung her head.

'And you, Mr Grimes,' the inspector added. 'I'll need a statement.'

'Of course, Inspector,' I told him.

Outside, the barking had become a hysterical cacophony of fierce snarling and desperate howling. Inspector Clackett turned and bellowed in the direction of the sound.

'Mulroney! Barstow! If you can't get that damned hound under control, then shoot it!'

'No, don't do that!' I protested. 'I'm good with dogs, Inspector. Let me see if I can control it.'

Call me soft-hearted but, savage as the Moravian boarhound seemed, it was a pedigree dog which had clearly been mistreated, and didn't deserve a bullet in its skull.

'It's all the same to me,' said Inspector Clackett with a shrug. 'Just get it out of here and then report to me at the station in Hibernian Yard, understood?'

I told him that I did.

Ordering his constables to remove the body, the inspector placed Clarissa in a pair of handcuffs and led her outside, through the gawping crowds, to the police carriage. She seemed like a broken woman.

'Tell Tilly that I won't be home for luncheon,' she said with a barely suppressed sob.

I watched them go before crossing the blood-red studio to the back door. With shaking fingers, I gripped the door handle.

As I did so, there was a colossal *thud*, followed by scraping and splintering as the dog's claws scratched at the wood. Low, menacing snarls sounded from outside. I swallowed hard, turned the handle and eased the door open.

The Moravian boarhound had been muzzled by the constables, and from his battered collar there hung the leash they'd attached before abandoning the struggle. I was just able to read a name on the strip of corroded metal that was attached to the leather collar, *Kaiser*, the fading letters etched in italic script. I stepped into the yard, and the dog flinched, obviously expecting a kick or a blow. I could make out matted patches of dried blood that suggested Laurence had beaten the dog, perhaps with that cane of his.

I held out a hand towards him and whispered softly.

'Kaiser, easy boy. I'm not going to hurt you ...'

I've always had a way with dogs – a kind of empathy and understanding, you could call it. I can tell just by looking into a dog's eyes what its temperament might be. Lady Ambrose's Penanganese lapdog, Frou-frou, for instance, had the black heart of a hellhound, while Lucky Bob, the champion Hightown racing whippet had the soul of a long-suffering saint.

Kaiser raised his muzzled snout and sniffed at my hand. I let him get my scent, then I knelt down and looked into the dog's eyes. They were large and pale caramel in colour, typical of a pedigree Moravian boarhound's. The bushy eyebrows gave him a questioning look. As our eyes met though, the low, throaty growling started up again, and the fur on the nape of his back stood on end.

'Kaiser,' I whispered. I held his gaze. The growling ceased and the dog took a step towards me. 'Good dog,' I said encouragingly.

I let him smell my hand again, and continued to whisper his name. His teeth were no longer bared and, behind the muzzle, his tongue lolled.

'Good boy!' I said again. This was no hot-blooded cur, at least, not by nature. Kaiser was a fine creature, every bit as noble as his name suggested. Beneath his violent exterior beat the loyal heart of man's best friend. I could tell by the look in his eyes.

I reached forward, the back of my hand to the dog's snout. His shoulders dipped and he came forward slowly and cautiously. The fur at his neck was standing on end, but he hadn't started growling again, and the shaking was down to the slightest of tremors. He sniffed at my hand again, then, tail wagging, his tongue flicked through the metal bars of the muzzle and licked me.

Taking care not to make any sharp movements, nor to position my hand where he couldn't see it, I reached slowly forwards and ruffled the fur at the side of his neck. He licked me again, his tongue warm and soft.

'Good lad, Kaiser,' I whispered. 'You're safe now. Nobody's going to hurt you again . . .'

Despite his ill treatment, I could tell that Kaiser was a magnificent specimen. He had probably been the victim of a muttmonger, a dog thief specializing in holding expensive breeds for ransom. How he'd come into Laurence Oliphant's possession was something of a mystery, though in this disreputable part of town, not a very big one. Most lock-ups needed guard dogs for security, and their owners were seldom picky about where they came from. But it was a criminal waste of a dog as magnificent as Kaiser to turn him into a half-starved, savage guard dog.

I had a hunch. Although I realized that you can't teach an old dog new tricks, I hoped that those already learned might be revived.

'Sit,' I told him firmly.

Kaiser simply stood there.

'Sit!'

With a soft sigh, the great dog sat down on his haunches. He stared up at me.

'Good boy,' I told him.

I got him to lie down, then sit again, then to roll over, and I crouched down and tickled his tummy. Not only had Kaiser been trained, but he'd been trained well, and I wondered whether Laurence Oliphant had even bothered to find this out before locking him up in the dingy back yard and casually brutalizing the poor creature.

I picked up the leash and, standing up, patted Kaiser on the back. 'Come on, boy,' I said.

We set off through the side gate and made our way up the alleyway. Back on Blood Alley, we skirted round the crowd of fascinated onlookers still clustered at the front of the lock-up, and headed for Blue Boar Lane.

If Clarissa Oliphant and I had made an odd couple, then Kaiser and I were a good deal odder, with the huge dog – the size of a small pony – trotting obediently at my side and glancing up at me meekly from behind the police muzzle. With the dog now displaying both his pedigree and obvious good training, the brutal metal muzzle clamped round his head looked curiously incongruous.

'Good boy, Kaiser,' I said proudly as he trotted to heel. I patted his head. 'Good lad.'

I stopped off at Arnold's the local butcher's and purchased a pennyworth of offal, with a lamb bone thrown in for free, then bought a couple of glazed earthenware dishes from Eastwick's next door. Back at number 3 Caged Lark Lane at last, I led Kaiser through the archway to the back yard behind. It was large and airy, turfed behind a whitewashed fence and criss-crossed with clothes lines where the occupants of Caged Lark Lane dried their laundry. In the corner, by a stand of sunflowers, was the kennel where Disraeli, old Sergeant-Major Miller's pet terrier, had once lived.

'Your new home, Kaiser,' I told him.

It was a snug fit, but Kaiser seemed to take to it immediately, sniffing about before flopping down inside the kennel, his head and shoulders outside. I unstrapped the muzzle and ruffled the fur on his head, before turning to unpack my purchases.

Kaiser watched me expectantly, his head cocked to one side. I unwrapped the newspaper package and dropped the glistening innards into one of the dishes. Then I dunked the other dish in the water butt, and set both of them down before him. Kaiser climbed from the kennel, sniffed the food, then hesitated.

'Eat, lad,' I said. Tail wagging, he buried his long scarred snout in the bloody scraps and began wolfing them down. I dropped the bone beside him. 'The second course,' I said. 'I'm going out for a bit. Be a good boy.'

I walked to the police station in Hibernian Yard. Given the local constabulary's attitude to highstacking, I thought it best. I arrived half an hour later, climbed the steps to the two black entrance doors and went in. The clock on the wall opposite showed two o'clock.

'I'm here with regard to the death of Laurence Oliphant,' I told the sergeant at the desk. 'My name's Barnaby Grimes. Inspector Clackett asked me to make a statement.'

'Did he now?' the portly sergeant said, scratching behind his ear with his pen. 'Then you'd better take a seat,' he added, nodding to a row of dark varnished benches that lined the green tiled walls of the vast, dingy entrance hall. 'Someone will be along presently.'

I took a seat and looked about me. The benches were full of the usual suspects. There were petty pickpocket dandies wearing decorated waistcoats and expressions of injured innocence, and protesting chorus girls in gaudy dresses and too much make-up. River-toughs from the docks and gang members from Gatling Quays eyed each other mistrustfully, while black-gowned lawyers and slick-haired clerks of the court strode purposefully past, clutching armfuls of yellowing documents tied up with red ribbons. I took off my coalstack hat, folded it up and settled down to wait.

Four hours later, I was still waiting. People had come and gone, striding through the hall in ones and twos, and disappearing into the various rooms which led off it. Once a large family of eight circus entertainers, including several shame-faced clowns escorted by two constables, had been ushered into the hall at the end. But no one came for me. Even when I reintroduced myself to the new sergeant on duty at the desk, and had been assured that someone would be soon be with me, no one came.

Only when, at six o'clock, having decided to leave, I climbed to my feet and headed for the door, did someone call my name. I turned to see Inspector Clackett standing with his hands on his hips, looking at me.

'You're the tick-tock lad, aren't you?' he said dismissively. I nodded. 'Follow me.'

The interview took place in a small,

windowless room that I took to be his office. There was a roll-top desk overflowing with paperwork in one corner and two high-back chairs on either side of a low baize-covered table. The walls were decorated from floor to ceiling with plaster death masks of convicted murderers, giving the gloomy chamber an intensely sinister atmosphere.

Inspector Clackett pulled up a chair and sat down, gesturing for me to sit down in the chair opposite.

'Don't mind them,' he said with an unpleasant smile, as he noticed me eyeing the ghostly faces around us. 'They're my testimonials, Mr Grimes. Because you see' – his deep-set eyes narrowed – 'Clackett always gets his man. Or, in this case, woman.' He cleared his throat. 'Now, what can you tell me about the murder of Laurence Oliphant, Mr Grimes?'

As he picked up a quill and a sheet of paper, I told him all about how Clarissa Oliphant and my paths had first crossed; about the

Inspector Clackett pulled up a chair and sat down . . .

assignment she had given me, as well as the fee she had paid, and I detailed my initial findings. It soon became apparent, however, that Inspector Clackett was most interested in the events that had taken place at 12 Aspen Row the previous evening. With his hooked nose thrust forward, he probed my memory, encouraging me to recall everything that I'd overheard. And, though I didn't intend to, with every word I uttered, I fear I made Clarissa Oliphant seem more guilty.

'You say she was controlling,' he pressed.

'I said *Laurence* accused her of controlling him,' I countered.

The inspector nodded. 'Accused her of snooping and prying into his affairs. Claimed she treated him like a wayward child. And yet,' he went on, 'she refused to lend him money – money she has through an inheritance,' he added, spitting out the word as though it was something distasteful, 'left to her by the late Lord Riverhythe . . .'

'A strongbox full of gold sovereigns, Laurence said,' I told him.

'Indeed,' he said, 'sovereigns she refused to lend to her brother, which apparently prompted him to steal an item of some value, to wit a . . .' He paused, licked his finger, and flicked through the pages of his notebook. 'A Dalmatian duelling sabre.' He looked up. 'The murder weapon.'

I swallowed. 'As I said, Inspector, I'd seen it hanging above the mantelpiece. Laurence must have taken it down . . .'

'Yet you did not see him leaving with it,' the inspector said. 'Nor have you any knowledge of what Miss Oliphant did following your departure at . . .' He paused again. 'At eight forty-five.'

'No, but—'

He raised his hand to silence me. 'Furthermore,' he continued, 'when you visited her at eight o'clock this morning, you claimed that Miss Oliphant looked as if she had not slept all night.' He shook his head, his fleshy jowls quivering. 'It doesn't look good for Miss Oliphant, does it?' he said.

It certainly didn't, and I clearly wasn't helping the redoubtable duelling governess either. Inspector Clackett sat back in his chair, hands clasped behind his head and a self-satisfied expression on his face.

'Read the statement through, Mr Grimes,' he said. 'Then sign it.'

Written down, my words seemed even more damning of Clarissa Oliphant, yet they were a true enough representation of what I'd said. Regretfully, I signed my name.

'What happens now?' I asked.

'Now?' said Inspector Clackett, leaning forward. 'You're free to go, Mr Grimes. Your presence will, of course, be required in court at a future date, of which you'll be informed in due course.'

'And Miss Oliphant?' I asked.

'Miss Oliphant?' the inspector repeated.

'Miss Oliphant will be charged with the murder of her brother, Laurence Oliphant, and stand trial. Until then, she will be an inmate of Whitegate Model Prison.'

CHAPTER 7

I knew of Whitegate Model Prison by reputation. It was a new prison, built to a revolutionary design based on the beliefs of Jeremy Hobholt, one of the great thinkers of the age. Unlike the old prisons like Gallowgates and Highheath, with their crowded communal cells, this model prison was a so-called panoptican.

It was octagonal in shape, three storeys in height and with a central viewing platform from which the warders could observe the inmates. But the most revolutionary aspect of Whitegate was that these inmates were kept in solitary confinement, in individual cells, and forbidden to talk at all times. Even in the exercise yard, they were made to wear hoods so the inmates could not fraternize with, or even see, their fellow prisoners.

Hobholt firmly believed that this allowed each prisoner to reflect on their crimes and aided their reformation. That, however, was not what I'd heard. Rumour abounded of inmates of Whitegate being driven mad by the rigidly enforced isolation and silence of the place, and being transferred to the lunatic asylum at Watermeadows Lane.

Clarissa Oliphant, I knew, would find it hard being locked up there. Visiting times for those awaiting trial were strictly limited and there was no way I would be allowed to see her, the inspector had informed me, until Monday morning at the earliest. In the meantime, though, there was someone I needed to visit.

Clarissa's parlourmaid, Tilly.

I imagined that the poor girl would be desperate with worry at the disappearance of her mistress, and I set off for Aspen Row at once. Ducking down the first alley I came to, I shinned up a conveniently placed drainpipe and onto the tiled rooftops. Night had fallen, cold and foggy, while I'd been stuck inside the police station. My rather threadbare jacket did little to keep me warm, and I was missing my poacher's waistcoat. Fifteen minutes later, however, having dashed across the rooftops at breakneck speed, I reached my destination with sweat beading my forehead.

I raised my cane and was about to rap on the door, when I heard the sounds of muffled sobbing coming from inside.

'Tilly?' I said, knocking firmly and shouting through the letter box. 'Tilly, it's me, Barnaby. Let me in.'

'Barnaby,' I heard her say. 'Thank goodness.'

Footsteps came running across the hallway, followed by the sound of bolts and a chain being released. The door flew open, and Tilly threw herself at me.

'It's all right,' I told her, hugging her tightly. You're safe now. Tell me what happened.'

She pulled away and looked up at me, her blue eyes red-rimmed, and her pretty cheeks stained with tears. She pushed her hair away from her face.

'I . . . I was so frightened, Barnaby, and it got later and later, and the mistress didn't come back,' she fretted, the words stumbling over each other. 'And she still isn't here, and she's never out this late. And then I heard sounds upstairs, and I thought she was back and had slipped in without my noticing, but when I looked, there was no one there, and . . .'

I squeezed her hands. 'You've been very brave, Tilly,' I told her, 'but I'm afraid I've got bad news.'

I stepped inside, closing the door behind me, and led her through to the cosy kitchen, with its copper pots and blazing range. I sat her down in the rocking chair and told her what had happened. Tilly gasped and buried her face in her hands.

'Mr Oliphant, dead,' she whispered. 'And the mistress accused of his murder! Oh, what is a poor maid-of-all-work to do, Barnaby?' Tilly sobbed.

Just then, there came the soft creaking of a loose floorboard from upstairs. Tilly looked up, her eyes wide with terror.

'There it is again,' she said. 'I told you, Barnaby.' She swallowed. 'I didn't imagine it.'

'Leave this to me,' I told her. 'You stay here.'

I drew my sword, left the kitchen and crept up the carpeted stairs as quietly as I could. Peering inside from the landing, I could see that what I took to be the door to Clarissa Oliphant's bedroom was open. Drawers had been pulled out, cupboard doors hung open, and various items lay strewn across the floor. The room had clearly been searched, and pretty thoroughly by the look of it.

The adjacent room was at the back of the house, directly above the drawing room. It was where I'd heard Laurence Oliphant pacing about on my first visit. The door was closed, and I paused and pressed my ear to the dark-stained wood. Silence. I waited for a moment or two, then, gripping my sword firmly, I seized the door handle and marched into Laurence Oliphant's bedchamber.

I looked around. There was a wall lamp to the right of the door. I pulled a box of vestas from my pocket, struck one and lit the gas. As I adjusted the mantle, a golden yellow glow filled the air, banishing the shadows to the corners of the room – but failing to reveal any intruder lurking there. Nevertheless, I felt ill at ease, every fibre of my body tense and braced as I took in my surroundings.

Unlike the rest of the house, Laurence Oliphant's bedchamber was stark, with bare boards and empty walls. Heaps of boxes and crates stood piled up on both sides of the room, with various pieces of what I took to be photographic equipment nestling between them. Everything was covered in a thin layer of dust, and a faint tang of chemicals hung in the air.

Beneath the window at the far end of the room was a small metal-framed bed, with crumpled blankets strewn across a thin mattress. An easel stood at the end of the bed behind a varnished wooden screen. It had what looked like a painting propped up against its angled struts. My curiosity aroused, I went to inspect it more closely and was surprised to discover that it wasn't an oil painting at all, but a photographic image mounted on thick card. I pulled the easel round until the lamp glow fell upon the picture.

The big ears and small eyes. The snub nose. A strand of silvery hair that had come free from the bun and hung down across a fleshy cheek. The high-collared jacket, buttoned at the neck . . .

It was the likeness of Clarissa Oliphant, captured in a beautifully modulated black and white image. But it wasn't just her features and clothes that I recognized, it was her expression. The lofty superiority of her steady gaze. The parsimonious tightness in her lips. It was as though I wasn't merely looking at a likeness of Clarissa Oliphant, but at the essence of the woman herself. It was more life-like than any painting I'd ever seen.

I leaned forward, my sword lowered. Laurence Oliphant's looped signature filled the bottom left-hand corner; below it, there was a date. The picture, I realized, was over a year old, with the image as crisp as the day it had been produced.

'An oliphantype,' I murmured.

As if in response, I heard a faint hissing noise, like the expelling of air. My body tensed. I spun round, brandishing my sword, but the room was empty.

Just then, in the flickering glow of the lamplight, and for the briefest of moments, I thought I glimpsed a half-formed, spectral shape by the doorway. It was translucent and indistinct, yet there was the suggestion of the tip of an ear, the curve of a shoulder.

'Barnaby!' It was Tilly, calling up from the foot of the stairs. 'Barnaby, are you all right?'

Suddenly, the door slammed shut. The next moment, Tilly screamed, her cries of terror echoing round the empty house.

'Tilly!' I shouted back. 'Tilly, I'm coming!'

I hurtled across the room, tore the door open and dashed along the landing. From the top of the stairs I could see her. She was lying at the foot of the stairs, her mobcap beside her and her hair unpinned. I slid swiftly down the banister, and landed beside her.

'Oh, Ba . . . Ba . . . Barnaby,' she stammered, looking up. Her sobs caught in her throat as I helped her shakily to her feet. 'Something brushed past me. It knocked me aside.'

'That's the thing,' she said, her face taut with fear. 'I didn't see anything, Barnaby.'

'It?' I said. 'What did you see?'

'That's the thing,' she said, her face taut with fear. 'I didn't see anything, Barnaby.'

Just then, more sounds came from the drawing room. I pulled away from Tilly and, sword before me, raced across the hall. I burst into the room and froze. Behind me, Tilly let out a little cry.

The large sash-window that led out into the back garden was open, and the curtains were flapping in the wind. I strode across the floor and pulled the window down with a rumbling thud. I fastened the catch.

'Whatever it was,' I told her, 'it appears to have gone now.'

'Look, Barnaby! Look!' Tilly's horrified voice sounded from behind me.

I turned to see her staring at the wall opposite the window. The landscape painting that would have hung there was propped up against the wainscoting beneath, while the strongbox it had concealed was open, the heavy iron door hanging back on its hinges, and a key protruding from its lock.

'What was in it?' I asked.

Tilly turned to me, her face white with shock. 'The mistress's gold sovereigns,' she said, confirming what I'd feared. 'Her inheritance from Lord Riverhythe!' Her face crumpled. 'It was her nest egg, Barnaby. She depended on it, and now it's gone. She's ruined!'

CHAPTER 8

There was no question of Tilly staying in the Oliphants' residence after the strange events of that night, and I escorted her to her aunt's house in Mulberry Court, not far from my rooms in Caged Lark Lane. Despite the lateness of the hour, one look at her niece's terrified face convinced the old fishwife that this was indeed an emergency, and she was happy to take her in.

I returned to my rooms, exhausted and disturbed by the day's events in equal measure, and went straight to bed. I fell almost immediately into a deep sleep, only to be plagued by nightmares of a hideous apparition emerging from the lock-up and pursuing me down Blood Alley. Suddenly, I was cornered, and it pressed its appalling face close to mine, its fetid breath suffocating me. I tried to raise my hands, to push away the unseen head that was pressing closer and closer into my face. But I couldn't move. I couldn't get away.

I felt something wet graze my chin and draw slowly up my grimacing face; over my nose, across my forehead. Then again. And again . . .

My eyes snapped open. 'Kaiser!' I exclaimed.

The dog cocked its head to one side, then leaned forward for another lick.

'Kaiser! Down, boy!'

Shamefacedly, the huge hound stepped down from the bed and sat on the floor, staring back at me expectantly. I sat up and patted his head, then glanced across at my clock.

It had seemed like a good idea the night

before, having the guard dog in my attic rooms, sleeping on a blanket by the door. Now, wide awake at only half past six on a Sunday morning, I was beginning to regret my decision. Rolling over and going back to sleep was out of the question. I pushed the covers back and climbed out of bed.

'Just give me half an hour,' I told the dog, 'and I'll take you for a walk.'

I don't know for certain whether the creature recognized the word *walk*, but his tail started thumping noisily against the floor. I washed and dressed quickly, and was putting the kettle on to boil when there was a soft knock at the door.

My heart missed a beat, and I had to remind myself that, as a general rule, phantoms don't knock on doors. With Kaiser standing alert at my side, I unlocked the door and opened it.

'Barnaby,' came a familiar voice, and Will Farmer, his wheelboard clamped under one arm, stepped into the room. 'I thought . . . '

His gaze fell on the dog. Grinning broadly, he crouched down and looked into the dog's eyes. 'And who are *you*?' he said, stroking and patting his head, and then laughed as Kaiser licked his face and neck.

'His name's Kaiser,' I told him. 'He belonged to Laurence Oliphant, the brother of that client I was telling you about. The *late* Laurence Oliphant,' I added.

Will looked up in surprise.

'Laurence Oliphant has been murdered,' I told him. Just then, a low, flutey whistle filled the air as the kettle came to the boil. 'We'll have a cup of tea,' I said, 'and I'll tell you all about it.'

Will Farmer seemed bemused as I outlined the bizarre events of the previous day. He shook his head as he placed his cup back on its saucer.

'Who do you think the intruder at the Oliphants' house was?' he asked, his eyes wide with wonder.

I'd witnessed more than my share of the supernatural over the years, from werewolves and evil skulls to a legion of undead zombies, and I'd learned to keep such things to myself as much as possible. It didn't do to go about scaring the good citizens of this great city any more than one had to.

'I'm not sure,' I told Will, 'but I plan to find out, starting first thing Monday morning.' I stretched and yawned extravagantly. 'Now, what plans do you have for this fine day of rest?'

Will grinned. 'Since it's Sunday,' he said, tapping the wheelboard, 'I was going for a spin in Centennial Park, and I wondered if you'd like to join me.'

'Excellent idea,' I said, 'and I'll bring Kaiser. He could do with a good run.'

We set off ten minutes later, with Will babbling on about the fine adjustments he'd been making to that wheelboard of his, as well as the various moves he was beginning to perfect. The early morning mist was soon burned off by the autumn sun, leaving the streets pink and golden, though still bitterly cold. At the bottom of Waverley Avenue, Will took a left turn.

'I thought we were going to Centennial Park,' I said.

'We are,' Will replied, and grinned sheepishly. 'But I thought I'd see whether Molly fancied accompanying us. It's such a lovely morning.'

'Molly Gosney?' I said, twitching Kaiser's leash to stop him pulling ahead. 'What makes you think she might be interested in you?'

Will's grin broadened. 'Because she told me herself,' he said, and winked. 'At the Alhambra music hall last night . . .'

'Why, you sly old rascal,' I said, throwing back my head and laughing.

As we rounded the corner of Prospect Avenue, *Gosney and Daughter* homed into view. The shop was shut up and in darkness, but when Will rang the bell, Molly soon appeared at the door to let us in.

'Will,' she said, blushing charmingly. 'And Mr Grimes.'

'Call me Barnaby,' I told her.

'Barnaby,' she repeated and nodded. 'My mother's going to be very pleased to see *you*. She's just been putting the finishing touches to your poached egg waistcoat.'

Both Will and I burst out laughing. Molly stared at the pair of us, one after the other, her brow lined with confusion. 'What?' she said. 'What did I say?'

'It's a *poacher's* waistcoat,' Will explained, and kissed her lightly on her forehead.

'Well, whatever it's called,' said Molly primly. 'It's ready.'

She called up the stairs to her mother, who emerged a moment later, the newly completed waistcoat hanging over her arm. She smiled at me warmly, and gripping the garment by the shoulder seams and holding it out before her, crossed the shop floor towards me.

'I only hope it fits,' she said anxiously.

I removed my jacket and slipped the waistcoat on, and Mrs Gosney clucked and tutted as she did up the buttons at the front, tightened the buckle at the back, and smoothed down the shoulders. She turned me round and steered me towards a full-length mirror, where I paused and looked at my reflection.

The waistcoat was a work of art. Made of light-brown canvas and lined with buttery silk, it had been decorated with tooled leather corner-pieces and ten polished mother-of-pearl buttons. There were six numbered pockets stitched to one front panel, and eight to the other, with hooks, rings and tags stitched between them, and two more deep pockets on the inside – in short, a place for everything I needed, and more besides. Keys, pencils and notebook, documents, dockets and calling cards; there was even a handy pouch for the grit I carried for long rooftop jumps on frosty mornings. Best of all, the waistcoat fitted me perfectly.

'I don't know how to thank you,' I said.

'There's no need for thanks, Barnaby,' she said. 'It's the least I could do. We're so grateful to you for rescuing Bobbin, aren't we, Molly?'

But Molly hadn't heard. She and Will were by the door, staring into each other's eyes and giggling softly.

'Come on, you two,' I said, slipping my jacket over my fine new waistcoat. 'I thought we were going wheelboarding.'

It was mid morning by the time the four of us reached Centennial Park. The russet leaves of the trees were stark against the deep-blue sky and, as we passed beneath the cast-iron arch entrance, I saw that the fine weather had attracted crowds. The place was thronging.

There were men with dogs, elegant couples walking arm in arm, and clusters of nannies with sleek black perambulators. Young children flew gaudy kites, rolled wooden hoops and prodded at sailboats which bobbed about on the ornamental lake. Half a dozen older boys were playing tag rounders, using their jackets for bases and tackling each other to the ground; while twin sisters, each in matching sailor suits, shrieked with delight as they rolled down a grassy hill – much to the annoyance of their over-protective governess.

Will dropped his wheelboard to the ground, jumped onto it and, scooting with one leg, propelled himself along the path towards the bandstand. Molly and I ran after him, while Kaiser, on the end of his leash, bounded along before us. Will skidded round, and brought the wheelboard to a standstill. His cheeks were red with a mixture of cold air and exhilaration.

'Your turn, Barnaby,' he said eagerly.

I handed Kaiser's leash to him and stepped gingerly onto the board, which immediately shot forward, out of control, pitching me down to the ground – and causing both Will and Molly to howl with laughter. Kaiser lowered his head and licked my face where I lay.

'It's all a matter of balance,' Will told me, as I prepared myself for a second attempt. 'Keep your legs flexed, your knees bent and arms outstretched. You'll soon get the hang of it.'

I persisted and, thanks to the balance that highstacking had taught me, before long I was managing rides of twenty, thirty yards or more. Will was right. Wheelboarding *was* fun. Lots of fun. What was more, not only were people pausing to watch us, fascinated by the curious wheeled contraption, but some were even stopping to ask Will where they could buy a wheelboard of their own. Maybe it would become all the rage after all.

'I think you've got the hang of it, Barnaby,' Will told me. He turned to Molly, a smile on his lips. 'Do you think he's ready yet?'

'Oh, yes,' said Molly, her dark eyes flashing with amusement.

Will nodded and grinned at me. 'We think it's time you had a shot at Cheese-Chaser Hill.'

I swallowed nervously. Cheese-Chaser Hill was the steepest incline in the park. It was where, every July, a cheese-chasing competition would take place. At the blast of the alderman's whistle, a round truckle of cheese would be rolled down the hill and dozens of the city's most reckless young men would chase after it, running and tumbling down the hill in an attempt to get to the bottom first – and there were always several who ended up in St Jude's Hospital with broken bones.

Still, pleased with my success so far, I decided to give it a go. I patted Kaiser and began the long tramp up the steep slope, the wheelboard clamped under one arm. I was about halfway up when an involuntary

shudder gripped my body, as though someone had walked over my grave.

I looked round nervously, but I was quite
alone.

I continued climbing, but the feelings
of unease persisted. The hairs at the nape of
my neck were standing on end, and despite
my new lined waistcoat I felt shivery and
gooseflesh-cold.

Behind me, I heard Kaiser barking. I turned
and peered down the hill. He was straining
at the leash, desperate to break free, his
anguished yelps and howls echoing round the
park. Will and Molly were beside him, trying
their best to calm him down, but the dog was
inconsolable.

Whatever had spooked me was clearly
unsettling Kaiser as well.

Reaching the top of the hill, I turned
and placed the wheelboard at my feet and
prepared myself for the descent. In the
distance, Kaiser was struggling more

frantically than ever to break free, up on his back legs and barking furiously.

'It's all right, lad,' I said softly. 'I'm coming.'

With that, I leaped onto the wheelboard and propelled myself down the hill. I kept my legs flexed, my knees bent and my arms outstretched, just as Will had instructed. And as I gathered speed, I felt the wind tugging at my jacket and blowing through my hair. Apart from highstacking, it was the most exhilarating thing I'd ever done.

Ahead of me, Will and Molly were shouting encouragement and waving at me, their arms raised high above their heads. As for Kaiser, the poor creature looked petrified. His fur was bristling, his eyes rolled, and from behind his bared teeth there came a sustained, high-pitched snarl.

The next moment, there was a splintering crack, and the wheelboard flipped forward on itself, catapulting yours truly high up

With that, I leaped onto the wheelboard and propelled myself down the hill.

into the air. I somersaulted over and landed heavily on my back, where I lay, badly winded.

I opened my eyes to see Will and Molly staring down at me, a mixture of concern and glee on their faces.

'Are you all right?' said Will.

I pulled myself up on my elbows. 'Nothing broken,' I said.

'You must have hit a bump or something,' said Will. He handed me Kaiser's leash and checked his wheelboard for damage. Finding none but a single bent spoke, he looked up. 'Come on, Barnaby,' he said, 'I'll treat us all to roasted chestnuts.'

The four of us crossed the path to the glowing brazier next to the bandstand, where a grizzled old man was selling chestnuts in brown paper cones. As we approached, the heat from the coals blasted in our faces. The old man looked up, the fiery glow gleaming on his silvery stubble and peg-like teeth.

'Three bags, sir,' said Will, handing over three copper coins.

Kaiser had calmed down, his fur lying flat at his shoulders and his tongue lolling as he sniffed at the chestnuts. We sat down on our jackets and set to work on the chestnuts, and the air filled with their rich, earthy smell as we peeled off the blackened skins. As my mouth filled with the sweet, pulpy flesh inside and I fed Kaiser a peeled chestnut in turn, the sunny park and its cheerful inhabitants banished all thoughts of spirits and phantoms from my head. It was a perfect Sunday in the park.

That night, with Kaiser curled up on his blanket, I plunged into a deep and dreamless sleep the moment my head hit the pillow, waking the following morning at seven o'clock with the light streaming in at my attic window.

Kaiser was already awake, gnawing softly at the mutton bone I'd given him the night before. When he saw that I was also awake, he climbed to his feet and trotted over to me. I cupped his great head in my hands and tickled him round the ears.

'I'm afraid it's the kennel for you this morning,' I told him. 'I have to go to White-gate Prison to pay Clarissa Oliphant a visit.'

The fine weather of the weekend had broken and, as I made my way across the rooftops that Monday morning, a light drizzle began to fall. I arrived at the prison gates shortly before ten o'clock. Visiting hours were between ten and twelve, and I joined the end of a desultory line of friends and relatives of the inmates awaiting trial and locked up inside. Convicted prisoners, follow-ing Jeremy Hobholt's rules, were allowed no visitors at all.

At ten on the dot, a low door set into one of the huge, white gates swung open, and a bulky prison warder appeared from the shadowy interior, an open book clutched in red, beefy fingers. The line began to shuffle forward, with the warder ticking off names on the page.

'Inmate to be visited?' he asked gruffly, without looking up, when I reached the front of the line.

'Clarissa Oliphant,' I told him.

He made a note in his book. 'And you are?'

'Barnaby Grimes. Tick-tock lad.'

Another note followed before I was allowed to enter.

A tall, heavily built warden with a jagged scar through one eyebrow led me silently into a small hall. It had a high vaulted ceiling, and a stone floor where a dozen square tables had been laid out in two rows. Most were already occupied, and the air buzzed with the low, intimate conversation forbidden in the rest of the prison. I was ushered to an empty table near the side of the hall and told to wait.

I shivered. The whitewashed walls and cold

stone floor combined with the vigilant prison warders to create an atmosphere of extreme oppressiveness. When the warder returned, he was accompanied by the stooped, shuffling figure of Clarissa Oliphant.

I smiled up at her, trying to disguise my shock at her appearance. Her face looked taut and drawn, her cheeks hollow and eyes ringed with dark circles. There were oily stains down the front of her dress, and I knew how the usually impeccably turned out woman must have hated my seeing her looking so dishevelled. The warder indicated the chair opposite me, and as Clarissa moved forward to sit down, there was a clanking of chains, and I realized her ankles were in manacles.

'Oh, this is awful, quite awful, Mr Grimes,' she said, her voice close to tears, the moment the warder withdrew. 'I had no idea how punishing these so-called "model" prisons actually are.'

She looked round sheepishly at the warder,

aware that raising her voice above a whisper would terminate our visit instantly.

'Thank you, Barnaby, for visiting me in this dreadful place. Needless to say, with the police convinced of my guilt, I'm in desperate need of your help.' She looked at me beseechingly. 'It goes without saying, I shall reward you handsomely for your efforts . . .'

I didn't have the heart to tell the old governess that, since the robbery at her house, she was virtually penniless.

'I'll do whatever I can,' I reassured her, taking my notebook from the second pocket of my new poacher's waistcoat. 'Now, did Laurence have any enemies? Anyone who might have wanted to see him dead?'

'I've thought of little else since my incarceration,' said Clarissa, struggling to keep her voice down, 'and there are four names that I keep coming back to. Although, due to Laurence's secretive nature, I know precious little about them . . .'

'And they are?' I urged, pencil poised above my notebook.

'First is Sir Crispin Blears,' said Clarissa. 'The noted society portrait painter. I know Laurence approached him for funds, but then, for reasons I can only guess at, accused him of attempting to destroy his life.'

She shook her head.

'Laurence was so highly strung, Barnaby, and his work only seemed to intensify his feelings of resentment . . . Then, of course, there was a chemist he seemed to blame for his unfortunate accident. Laurence actually claimed that this fellow had caused it on purpose, and was trying to kill him for some reason. A.G. Hoskins Industrial Chemists – I found a docket in Laurence's fustian weave overcoat once . . .'

Clarissa's eyes brimmed with tears.

'And the third name,' I pressed, aware that the warder was looking in our direction.

'Yes, yes, the third name,' said Clarissa,

gathering herself together with considerable difficulty. 'That unfortunately is Miles Morgenstern, my brother's former assistant. Laurence was ill, Barnaby,' she pleaded, her voice raised. 'And his accursed work was causing it . . .'

The warder was rapidly approaching our table as Clarissa continued, her voice now booming.

'And the fourth is his tutor, Dean Henry Dodson!' Clarissa exclaimed tearfully. '*He* started poor Laurence on this road to ruin! Go and see him, Barnaby,' she begged me as the warder took her by the arm and forcibly dragged her away, 'and demand that *he* explain himself!'

CHAPTER 9

The mansions of Monrovia Walk and Batavia Park, with their ivy-clad loggias, glass-roofed ateliers and ornate studios, were as distinctive and decorative as the grand society painters and sculptors who lived and worked in them. Classical villas and Mesopotamian follies nestled beside Byzantine palaces and miniature Bavarian castles, as each artist attempted to outdo his neighbours with his superior taste and artistic vision.

A brass plaque bolted to the wall of number 16 Batavia Park, a mosaic-encrusted mansion built in the Moorish style, confirmed that I'd reached the grand residence of the first name on the list I'd made of Clarissa Oliphant's prime suspects.

Sir Crispin St John Blears, FRSA

I pulled the bell rope. No sooner had the bell begun to jangle than the carved sandal-wood door opened, and I was confronted by a richly clad figure.

'Well, you're certainly not Lady Lavinia,' proclaimed a bored, foppish voice with a hint of disdain.

Sir Crispin Blears was a tall, aristocratic-looking man with a long face and an aquiline nose beneath a black mane of studiously ruffled hair, which had a single, distinctive white streak at its centre. Dressed in the long, flowing robes of an eastern potentate, anywhere else, Sir Crispin would have cut an absurdly comic figure. Yet here, in the doorway of this eccentric mansion, he seemed perfectly in keeping.

'Excuse the intrusion, sir,' I said. 'My

name's Grimes, Barnaby Grimes, and I've been commissioned, in a private capacity, to look into the affairs of the late Laurence Oliphant . . .'

'A swag-hound, eh?' snorted Sir Crispin.

It was a term used to describe private investigators who looked into unsolved crimes in the hope of reward money, or 'swag'. They were a disreputable bunch, little more than petty swindlers and blackmailers themselves, often implicated in the very crimes they claimed to be investigating.

'No, I assure you,' I protested, 'I'm a tick-tock lad by profession, and I'm looking into this as a favour to a client of mine.'

'The *late* Laurence Oliphant, you say?' said Sir Crispin, his eyes narrowing. 'A gifted fellow if, ultimately, a misguided one. Fortunately for you, Mr Grimes, my client is delayed,' he said, pulling a gold fob-watch from beneath his silken robes. 'You've got five minutes. Follow me.'

He took me up a sweeping staircase, the tiled walls lined with gold-framed portraits of various sizes. At the first-floor landing, he strode through an arched doorway and into a high-ceilinged studio.

It was cluttered with the tools of his trade – exotic rugs, animal skins and tapestries in one corner provided the backdrops to his portraits, while the tables and cabinets around the walls groaned beneath a bewildering array of props. There were tooled breastplates, plumed helmets, muskets, swords and shields for those of his clients who saw themselves as men of action or warriors from a bygone age; musical instruments, astronomical tools and ancient vases and urns for the artistic. There was even a stuffed polar bear and a lion skin for intrepid explorers to pose beside. In the centre of the studio, beneath a north-facing skylight, was a raised dais, upon which a gilded throne had been placed, with several tiger skins draped over its gilded arms.

And opposite it, on an immense easel, was a large canvas with an unfinished portrait of a breathtakingly beautiful woman.

'How can I help you, Mr Grimes?' said Sir Crispin distractedly, gazing at the portrait. 'I haven't seen poor Laurence for months,' he went on. 'Not since our little falling out . . .'

'Falling out?' I said.

He picked up a brush from the table beside the easel and dabbed at the painting.

'Eighteen months ago, Laurence Oliphant came to me with an invention that he claimed would revolutionize portraiture – a process of photogravure, or "painting with light", as I have heard it called, that he'd named oliphantography. I admit I was intrigued. I knew how the old masters had used mirrors and lenses to create projections on their canvases, and thought this new process might prove helpful. I became his backer, financing his experiments to the tune of ten guineas a month.'

He picked up a brush from the table beside the easel and dabbed at the painting.

I nodded, impressed. It was a sizable sum.

'Of course, I knew that there was no real artistic merit in Laurence's work. The man was little more than a chemist, but he didn't seem to see it that way . . .' Sir Crispin's voice trailed away as he scrutinized his painting. 'Dear Laurence began to get ideas above his station. Started claiming that his "oliphantypes" were a new art form and would make painting obsolete! It was the talk of a madman.'

Sir Crispin turned to me, his eyes blazing.

'I have dedicated myself to my art. I studied at the best conservatoires in Europe. I learned from the great Reynaldo Bottacini to produce my own palette of colours, using cinnabar and cochineal for red, cadmium for yellow, arsenic for emerald green. Many was the long night I spent grinding lapis lazuli and azurite gems with a mortar and pestle to produce ultramarine of such vibrancy . . . Then this . . . this . . . *pharmacist*,' he said, spitting out the word, 'with his glass plates and chemicals, tells me that he will replace the unique perspective of an artist's eye with a mechanical lens . . . '

He shook his head, and put the back of his clenched fist dramatically to his brow.

'I wanted nothing more to do with him,' he said. 'I stopped his monthly stipend two months ago in order to put an end to his outlandish boasts once and for all.' He turned back to the painting and dabbed at it angrily with his brush. 'Laurence didn't take it too well. Stormed out, muttering that I'd be sorry.'

I remembered the oliphantype of Clarissa Oliphant. It might have been produced with chemicals, but it had managed to capture something of the essence of the person; some internal truth. I suspected Crispin Blears, when he'd seen Laurence's work, had noticed it too.

'And that was the last time you saw him?' I said.

Sir Crispin turned. 'Well, yes, I suppose so . . .' he said uncertainly. 'Although there was the incident at the summer show at the Academy.' He paused, then laughed uneasily. 'Perhaps you read about it Mr Grimes. I was showing my portrait of Lady Sarah Poultney as Diana, goddess of the hunt, to quite considerable acclaim, when . . .'

'Yes?' I said, intrigued.

'The painting was damaged,' he said, his face colouring. 'Nobody saw it happen, although the gallery was well attended and the paintings watched at all times. But I suspected Laurence Oliphant was behind it.'

'Damaged?' I said. 'How?'

'The canvas was slashed, Mr Grimes,' he said hotly. 'With the point of a fencing sword by the look of it.'

Just then, I heard the doorbell jangle in the hallway below, followed by the low mumble of voices.

'That will be Lady Lavinia,' said Sir

Crispin, composing his face and returning the paintbrush to a jar on the table. 'I'm in my studio, Carruthers,' he called out, then turned to me. 'I'm afraid that's all I can tell you,' he said. 'But perhaps you can tell me something Mr Grimes. How exactly did poor Laurence die?'

I returned Sir Crispin's gaze levelly. 'He was murdered,' I told him, 'run through by a fencing sword.'

A.G. Hoskins Industrial Chemists was situated on Coldbath Road, a grubby back street not far from the wharves of Riverhythe, and a short walk from Laurence Oliphant's lock-up in Blood Alley. As I stepped through a low door situated next to a much larger set of double doors, a spring-loaded bell clanged above my head, announcing my arrival.

'Can I help you, sir?' said a thin, stooped-looking man with greasy hair and a grubby apron. Perched on top of his head was a tall stovepipe hat, to which were pinned scraps of crumpled paper – chits, dockets and formulae of various kinds by the look of them.

'Mr Albert Hoskins?' I asked, and received a nod in reply.

His brown eyes had a look of disappointment about them, an impression made stronger by his moustache, which drooped at the ends. It was as though fate had dealt him a bad hand, and he knew it.

'I'm enquiring into the affairs of the late Laurence Oliphant . . . ' I began, only for the chemist to stagger back from the low counter that separated us, like a head-butted bruiser in a bar-room brawl.

Albert Hoskins sank back onto a sack of desiccated phosphate granules, his head in his hands. Around us in the dismal light of the large warehouse were crates, sacks and huge jars of chemicals in powdered and liquid form, carefully stored and labelled on row upon row of wooden shelves.

'Mr Oliphant ... dead?' groaned the chemist. 'Well, I'll be blamed, no doubt about it. Old Albert's collar will be fingered, regardless of the facts of the case ...'

He gripped the brim of his stovepipe hat with both hands and pulled it down hard on his head, as if trying to take refuge inside it.

'So the explosion killed Mr Oliphant in the end, did it?' Albert peered up at me from beneath the brim of the hat with those disappointed eyes of his.

I was about to answer him, when the chemist continued, the words spilling out of his mouth in a spontaneous confession.

'Yes, I supplied Mr Oliphant with the chemicals he needed for his trade – and a strange mixture of powders and tinctures they turned out to be. Nitrates, iodides, naphtha and the like. Dangerous substances. Deadly substances if casually handled or mistakenly mixed. And I warned him, oh, how I warned him, but he took no notice. No, not him. He knew better, you see. He had a vision, a grand experiment; one day he and those precious "oliphantypes" of his would be famous . . . And he paid, in cash of course, up front for everything, until the explosion . . .'

The chemist paused, then rose from the sack, and came back to face me across the counter.

'Horribly burned, he was, when he came round after it happened. He accused me of adulterating my stock, mixing sawdust in my powders, vinegar in my tinctures . . . As if I'd do such a thing! Told me I'd be sorry, before he stormed off.

'Then I started noticing things going missing, stock running short, and just the same chemicals that I'd supplied Mr Oliphant with, though he was nowhere to be seen. So I took precautions, armed myself in case I caught him at it . . . Now he's gone and died of his burns!' he added mournfully. 'And I'll be blamed. Oh, yes, I'll be blamed!'

'Laurence Oliphant didn't die of his wounds,' I said, noticing the pair of pistols and an old cavalry rapier propped up against the chemist's side of the counter. 'He was murdered. Stabbed to death by a fencing sword.'

Miles Morgenstern was the next name on my list and, unlike Sir Crispin Blears in his flamboyant mansion and Albert Hoskins in his commercial premises, much harder to track down. Clarissa Oliphant had described him as Laurence's assistant, though when, with the aid of a local poultry merchant, I finally traced him to a small garret in a thin, rundown, six-storey house a few streets away from Blood Alley, Miles Morgenstern seemed to have set up in business for himself.

His name and title – *M. Morgenstern, Photo-Gravurist and Albumen Printer* – were etched onto one of a dozen small copper plaques screwed to the side of the front entrance. His business was on the top floor. I knocked on the chipped garret door, which was opened by a young man with curly red hair and round steel-rimmed spectacles which made his pale blue eyes appear to bulge.

'Miles Morgenstern?' I said. He nodded. 'Former assistant to Laurence Oliphant?'

The bulging pale blue eyes blinked twice. 'This is about Laurence's murder, isn't it?'

It was my turn to nod.

'The streets around here are awash with it,' he said. 'Every back-yard gossip is talking about it over the washing lines. I believe they've arrested his sister.' He paused and peered closely. 'But who are you?'

I told him that I was looking into the circumstances of her brother's murder on Clarissa Oliphant's behalf, which seemed to satisfy him, because he nodded.

'You'd better come in,' he said.

I followed him into a small, dark room with bare boards and sloping ceilings. It made my own modest rooms on Caged Lark Lane seem like a palace. Everything was crammed together, and seemed to have more than one use.

A single tin bowl doubled up as kitchen sink and wash basin. A mattress bolted to a plank of wood was a table during the day and a bed at night. His washing was draped from the wooden struts of a clothes dryer which hung from the ceiling, while a flat-topped stove beneath provided a means of cooking and dried his clothes at the same time.

'I always knew those chemicals would be the death of him,' Miles Morgenstern was saying as he removed a book and a glass of water, and pushed the bedside table across to me as a stool. 'I warned him often enough . . .'

'But aren't you in the same line of business?' I asked. 'The fixing of images from life using chemicals?'

'Oh, I am, Mr Grimes,' he said. He was perching on the corner of the table opposite me, his fingers picking at the mattress ticking beneath. 'But I use natural substances wherever possible. Gelatine and gum arabic. Egg white. Potato starch.'

I smiled to myself. Eggs and potatoes. It seemed that even his food had more than one use.

'Of course, there are some chemicals I can't do without,' he said, 'but I use ones that I can rely on, rather than Laurence's risky experiments.' He climbed to his feet. 'Perhaps I could show you, Mr Grimes.'

Unhooking a hanging lantern, he squeezed between the table and the stool, and opened a narrow door at the back of the room. I followed him, and found myself in a long thin attic, its sloping ceilings making me feel as though I was inside the hull of an upturned boat.

Worktops lined both walls, with shelves beneath and storage hooks above. There was a curious musty smell to the air, almost like a farmyard, and as I made my way sideways down the narrow galley, I thought I heard clucking – an idea confirmed when I came to a chicken coop with three feather-footed bantams pecking at the wire. This must have been how the poultry merchant two streets away came to have Morgenstern's address.

'You've discovered my girls,' said Miles Morgenstern with a throaty chuckle. 'Ruby, Alice and Maud.' He took a handful of millet and corn from a sack which hung from a hook above, and threw it inside the coop. 'It's the white from their eggs I use for my albumen prints.'

'Albumen prints?' I said. 'Not oliphantypes then?'

'Certainly not,' Miles Morgenstern said emphatically. 'I gave those up when I left Laurence to set up on my own. He didn't like it, but I felt I had to.' He pointed to the eggs. 'You must first beat the egg whites to a froth, then add a saturated solution of iodide of potassium. Thirty drops for each egg . . .'

As he spoke, Miles Morgenstern became more and more animated, his voice increasingly shrill. He was clearly enthralled by the process he was describing.

'What're those?' I asked, pointing to a rack of square plates of glass beside a large, empty vat.

'Those? Those, I coat with a gelatine mix,' he said. 'I make up large batches of the stuff in the vat there. A ratio of fifteen grains of Newton's patent opaque gelatine, to a two-ounce bottle of water, plus eighteen grains of bromide of potassium . . .'

I inspected the worktops as he continued what was rapidly becoming a lecture, making my way slowly past flat-bottomed trays, stoppered flasks, pairs of scales and racks of pipettes. I came to a pile of paper prints and held one up to the flickering yellow light.

It was the image of a serious-faced boy seated on an oversized armchair, his bony arms clamping a plump black and white Jack

Russell to his chest. The next was a picture of a street singer, her mouth open and eyes gleaming with passion. Next, a juggling clown, his blurred hands and the smear of thrown skittles making the picture look as though it was in motion, and after that a pretty girl wearing a mobcap and apron, a milk ladle in her hand . . .

I realized that Miles Morgenstern was standing at my shoulder. 'They're very good,' I told him.

'Thank you, Mr Grimes,' he said, his face glowing with pride. 'Every bit as clear and resonant as Laurence's oliphantypes, although he flew into one of his rages when I tried to get him to admit it. That was when I left his employ . . .'

'Did he often have these rages?' I asked.

'The chemicals he used to produce his oliphantypes were dangerous,' he said. '*Very* dangerous. I witnessed the damage they were causing.' He shook his head. 'Clouds of mercury vapour, cyanide, ether . . . Noxious toxins, Mr Grimes, all of them, and they did great damage to Laurence's personality.'

He shook his head regretfully, and frowned.

'When I first met him,' he went on thoughtfully, 'Laurence Oliphant was a quiet, mild-mannered man, generous and sympathetic to others. But as time passed, he became increasingly ill-tempered. Moody. Volatile. He would sulk morosely for hours, then explode into violent rage. He was always tired, but unable to sleep. He lost his appetite. And his hands, once so steady as they worked with the dangerous chemicals, developed a fine tremor that left him clumsy and accident-prone.' He turned and walked back along the attic. 'And every mishap he had would leave him more mistrustful and suspicious of those around him. Eventually, I found his rages and accusations intolerable, so I left and set up my own business – which is what you see before you.'

'How did Laurence view this competition?' I asked.

Miles Morgenstern smiled wryly. 'Much as I'd expected. He went berserk.' His brow furrowed. 'He shook his fist at me and shouted that I'd be sorry. It was the last time I saw him, although his premises are only a few streets away.'

We had reached the front door, which he pulled open. I stepped outside.

'Such a waste of a brilliant mind,' he mused. 'Such a terrible loss . . .'

I shook his hand and was about to set off down the stairs, when a thought occurred to me. I turned back.

'How did you become Laurence's assistant in the first place?' I asked.

'Oh, I thought you'd have known that,' Miles Morgenstern smiled good-naturedly, his blue eyes bulging from behind his spectacles. 'His sister, Clarissa, introduced me. You see, she was my governess in my younger days. She taught me to fence.'

Three names, three different stories, yet from my enquiries I'd learned that they were connected by Laurence Oliphant's sense of grievance against each of them. But there was a fourth name on the list that Clarissa Oliphant had given me; that of Dean Henry Dodson, Laurence's influential tutor at university.

The following day, I'd travelled up the river by flat-bottomed barge to the leafy banks and lawns of the ancient university Laurence had attended, and visited his old college. But all I could discover of Laurence's tutor was that he had gone on indefinite leave, a simple notice to this effect, written in his own hand, having been found nailed to the door of his study. The college authorities seemed remarkably untroubled by this turn of events. From what

I could gather, they disapproved of the dean's interest in photography – amongst other things – and seemed happy to see the back of him.

A firebrand orator and scourge of the university authorities, the dean attracted a loyal band of devoted followers from among the students he taught. These self-styled 'Dodson's Diehards' took their lead from the dean, experimenting in the ancient arts of alchemy and the occult, as well as the very latest fields of interest, such as photography. Most loyal and vocal of 'Dodson's Diehards', I discovered from a sleepy college bursar, was Laurence Oliphant himself, before he left the university to practise law.

Later on, as the bursar snored in his gatehouse, I slipped away and headed back to the city, placing a frayed card in the third left-hand pocket of my new poacher's waistcoat. It was the very card that had been nailed to Dean Henry Dodson's door, and that the bursar kept in a drawer of his desk:

*Have left on important business of a
personal nature. Will be gone some
considerable time.*
　　Dean Henry Dodson

It had been a busy few days, yet, as I turned
the corner of Caged Lark Lane and headed
for my rooms, I realized I was no nearer to
finding Laurence Oliphant's
murderer than I had been
when I left Clarissa
Oliphant in Whitegate
Prison. I was just about
to climb a drainpipe when
a newspaper vendor's
guttural cry made me stop
dead in my tracks.

'Read all about it! Tragic
death of high society painter!
Sir Crispin Blears killed!'

CHAPTER
10

Having bought a copy of the *Midtown Scrivener* from the paperlad on the corner, I entered number 3 Caged Lark Lane and headed up the stairs to my rooms in the attic. I slipped my key into the lock and heard the sound of Kaiser's warning bark, and opened the door to see the loyal creature standing in the middle of the room, staring at me. As he clapped eyes on me, his tail started wagging and he trotted towards me.

'Good lad,' I told him, ruffling his tousled head.

I was pleased he was there. After the day I'd had, I didn't feel like being alone. Once he was settled on the rug in front of a roaring coal fire, I pulled up an armchair, kicked off my highstacking boots and scrutinized the front page of the newspaper:

Sir Crispin Blears, renowned portrait painter and senior member of the Academy of Arts, was the victim of an accident outside his mansion in Batavia Park yesterday. According to eye-witness reports, the artist stepped out into the path of an oncoming coach and four, was severely trampled and then pinned beneath the rear wheels. Despite the ministrations of by-standers, including at least one physician and several fellow artists, the accident proved fatal.

Sir Crispin Blears was the son of Roland Blears, a noted tea importer, and first rose to prominence as a devoted student of Dean Henry Dodson of New College. After leaving university, he

*scored a notable triumph at the Academy
Summer Exhibition with his canvas, 'The
Battle of the Silesian Plains' ...*

Kaiser gave a contented sigh and rolled
over on the rug.

'Sleep well,' I whispered, placing the fire-
guard in front of the fireplace. 'Tomorrow,
you and I are going for a walk in Batavia
Park.'

The next morning, after sharing a frying pan
of breakfast sausages with my Moravian
boarhound, the two of us set off for Batavia
Park. Half an hour later, we arrived outside
Sir Crispin Blears' Moorish mansion.

A dark stain in the dusty street outside
marked the spot where the portrait painter
had met with his fatal accident – though a
restless night of tossing and turning had
convinced me that there was more to this
than met the eye, and I was anxious to inspect

the scene. As if to confirm my suspicions, I felt a hand on my shoulder and turned to see the frowning face of Sir Crispin Blears' butler, Carruthers.

'You're that tick-tock lad,' he croaked, 'that visited the master a few days ago.'

I confirmed to him that I was.

'The master was most unsettled following your visit, Mr Grimes, and no mistake,' the old butler told me, his brow furrowed with concern. 'Then the day before yesterday, I came into his studio and found him staring out of the window. All at once, he gave a cry of recognition and rushed out of the house. I went to the window, just in time to see a curious, hunched figure beckoning to him from the street. The master ran towards him and then . . .'

'And then, what?' I said.

Carruthers stared down at the stain in the dust.

'The master grasped the cloak the figure

wore,' he said, 'which seemed to come away in his hands, and I lost sight of the wearer. As I watched, the master, clutching the cloak, rose up in the air and then toppled into the street, just as the three o'clock post-coach galloped past . . .'

The old butler trembled. He was still clearly traumatized by what he had witnessed. I took him by the arm and guided him back towards his former employer's mansion.

'I don't suppose,' I said gently, 'that you have the cloak in question?'

Carruthers shuddered violently, then nodded. 'I prised the garment from my master's cold, dead hands, Mr Grimes, before the undertakers took his poor, broken body away.'

He entered the mansion and shuffled across the tiled hallway and through a door. Moments later, he returned holding a dusty, blood-stained cloak of worsted tweed. He handed it to me. Kaiser's disquiet increased, and he whined and snarled, his fur bristling as he sniffed the hem of the cloak.

'The police weren't interested, Mr Grimes,' Carruthers said ruefully. 'Dismissed my story as the ravings of an old retainer, no doubt. Simple accident, they maintained, and that's the story the papers all carried . . .'

Carruthers continued speaking in a low, mournful voice, but I was no longer listening. For as Kaiser tugged agitatedly on the end of his leash, I was staring at the label stitched into the collar of the cloak in my hands.

H. Dodson, it read.

So the cloak belonged to Dean Henry Dodson, the mysterious academic who had taught both Laurence Oliphant and Crispin Blears. Now, the pair he had tutored were dead, and the cloak clearly implicated the dean in the so-called accident that had killed Sir Crispin. I thought of the hideous face I'd glimpsed in the back window of Laurence Oliphant's lock-up. What if *that* had been

Dodson also? And what if *both* deaths had been by his hand?

All three men, in their different ways, had been involved with the new discipline of 'painting with light', and as PB had pointed out, squabbles were always breaking out between rival academics working in the same field. Perhaps Dodson had become envious and jealous of his former students, envying Crispin Blears' success and jealous of Laurence Oliphant's breakthroughs in photography.

I remembered the note the eccentric don had left on his study door. *Have left on important business ... Will be gone some considerable time ...* I was beginning to suspect he'd planned the whole thing, disappearing from the university and setting off for the city with murder in mind.

First Laurence, and now Sir Crispin Blears. Who would be next? I wondered, as I gazed at the blood-stained cloak in my hands.

Since the dean knew Laurence Oliphant and his pioneering work, he would also have met Laurence's assistant, Miles Morgenstern – or at the very least heard of his own work in photogravure. What was more, since Albert Hoskins was the primary supplier of the photographic chemicals that all of them required, there was every likelihood that Dodson also knew the owner of A.G. Hoskins Industrial Chemists . . .

I shivered as I remembered the burglary at Clarissa Oliphant's house the night after her brother's murder, and the strange presence I had sensed in his bedchamber. I'd felt it again in Centennial Park on that bright, cold Sunday morning when I fell from Will's wheelboard, and Kaiser had sensed it too.

'You lost sight of the wearer, you said,' I muttered, turning to the old butler.

'That's right, sir. The master grabbed the cloak and there was no one there,' Carruthers said. 'Whoever had been wearing it disappeared like . . . like . . .'

'A phantom,' I breathed.

I handed the cloak back to the open-mouthed butler. Then, tugging on Kaiser's leash, I left the Moorish mansion of the late Sir Crispin Blears and headed back down the broad, tree-lined thoroughfare of Batavia Park, my mind racing.

Albert Hoskins had told me of chemicals mysteriously going missing from his ware-house, and kept guns and a rapier behind his counter as a result. Sir Crispin Blears had told me his painting had been vandalized, and now he was dead.

Could Albert be in similar danger? I had to warn him, at the very least.

I headed off towards Gastown as fast as I could, with Kaiser trotting along beside me. Half an hour later we cut down Sleat Alley, which led to Coldbath Road, where the industrial chemist's was situated. We hurried along the shadowy alley, past a row of rundown workshops, the sounds of hammering, sawing and grinding mingling with the clatter of treadles and looms, and out onto the busy main street at the other end.

I paused and took my bearings. Diagonally opposite, on the corner of Coldbath Road and Tibbalds Lane, was the industrial chemist's premises. With Kaiser on a short leash, I waited for a brewer's dray to trundle past before darting out into traffic. I'd got halfway across the street when, all at once and without warning, a blinding white flash lit up the street, followed a second later by an ear-splitting blast.

For an instant, everything seemed frozen. There was a ringing in my ears, and the street around me was unnaturally still. Then everything started moving at once.

People were running in all directions, heads down and hands raised protectively over their heads. Horses reared up, whinnying and

pawing the air, while others bolted, their carts
and carriages lurching on the cobbles behind
them. Adults were shouting, children were
screaming, dogs barked and howled, while a
flock of startled pigeons rose up in a great
mass from the ledges and lintels of the
surrounding buildings. And ahead of me,
flames poured out of the shattered windows
of A.G. Hoskins Industrial Chemists as a fire
took hold, spreading through the building
and triggering explosion after explosion as
the volatile chemicals inside went up.

'Albert Hoskins,' I breathed, my worst fears
confirmed, as a tattered, blackened figure
appeared at the splintered doors, looking like
a sweep's apprentice fresh from a soot-
encrusted chimney, and stumbled into the
street.

Blood poured down from a gash at the side
of his head, soaking into his smoking shirt
front and torn apron and splashing onto the
paving stones. He managed half a dozen steps

. . . a tattered, blackened figure appeared at the splintered doors, looking like a sweep's apprentice . . .

before falling to his knees, then keeled over and collapsed on the ground. Dragging the leash of the trembling boarhound, I dashed towards him, picking my way between the wreckage of two upturned carts.

'Mr Hoskins,' I said, crouching down next to the injured chemist. 'Albert . . .'

His eyelids fluttered and he looked up at me, a mixture of pain and bewilderment in his gaze.

'There was someone there, I swear there was,' he gasped, wincing with every word. 'But when I looked, there was nobody . . .' His eyes widened. 'Then I saw it . . .'

I leaned forwards and cradled his head in my arms. 'What did you see?' I asked.

Albert Hoskins' brown eyes grew wider still, and he clutched at my sleeve. His lips parted, but nothing emerged except for a low gurgling sigh from the back of his throat. I put my ear to his mouth.

'The box of matches,' he whispered

desperately, 'floating in mid air, they were, and lighting themselves . . . Nothing I could do . . . to stop . . . the flames . . .'

Albert's eyes abruptly glazed over and I felt the tension in his body dissolve. His head slumped back.

I laid him gently down on the ground, swallowing hard. Just as I had feared, the phantom who'd murdered Laurence Oliphant and Sir Crispin Blears had struck again, and I had been powerless to prevent him. Now Albert Hoskins was dead. As I climbed to my feet, there was only one thought in my head.

Miles Morgenstern.

CHAPTER 11

'Come on, boy,' I said, tugging at Kaiser's leash.

The poor creature had been unnerved by the explosion and kept close to my side as the pair of us ran up Tibbalds Lane. Miles Morgenstern's garret was on Brazier Street, half a dozen or so roads away, and I kept to the less busy ones, darting from one to the next, my breath coming in puffy clouds.

The temperature had dropped sharply and the previous day's drizzle had turned to fine, grainy snow. By the time I arrived at the tall, thin building where Miles Morgenstern worked and lodged, the snow was beginning to settle.

With an unpleasant lurch of the stomach, I noticed that the front door was ajar. I pushed it open and was about to enter the dark hallway when Kaiser let out a bloodchilling howl and braced his front legs, refusing to enter.

'Come on, Kaiser,' I said. 'Heel, boy. Kaiser, *heel*!'

But the dog was having none of it. Fur ruffled and eyes rolling in his head, he whined pitifully and jerked back on the leash. I yanked it forward again. Suddenly it was tug-of-war, until all at once, with a resigned sigh, Kaiser stopped pulling.

'Good dog,' I said, and was reaching forward to pat him when, with a loud yelp, he leaped away. My shoulder jarred painfully in its socket, the leash slipped from my grip and I was left staring helplessly as the great hound bounded across the road. 'Kaiser!' I bellowed after him. '*Kaiser*!'

But the Moravian boarhound was oblivious to my calls. He dashed headlong into a narrow lane opposite and disappeared from view.

Something had spooked Kaiser, but there was nothing I could do for the moment, I told myself. I'd go in search of him just as soon as I had spoken to Miles Morgenstern. Yet as I walked along the gloomy hallway and up the flights of stairs, I too began to feel uneasy, my skin turning as cold and clammy as that of a freshly plucked goose.

I reached the eighth-floor landing to discover that the door to Miles Morgenstern's garret rooms was also open. It creaked softly when I pushed it, and I poked my head round the side and peered in.

'Hello?' I called out. 'Mr Morgenstern?'

There was no reply. I didn't like it, I didn't like it at all. Drawing my sword, I stepped cautiously inside.

The place looked abandoned, with a half-eaten plate of fried eggs and buttered bread at the end of the mattress-table and a pot of coffee bubbling on the stove. I crept across the floor and was turning off the gas when I heard a muffled thump from the other side of the door that led to his attic laboratory.

Now seriously alarmed, I crossed quickly to the door and opened it, only to freeze with shock.

Miles Morgenstern was before me, suspended in the air, his feet inches from the floor and his body shaking violently like a marionette in the clutches of an invisible puppet master. His face was bright purple and, as his steel-rimmed spectacles were dislodged and clattered to the floorboards, I saw his bloodshot eyes bulging from their sockets.

He was reaching up, his hands clawing at his throat as he gasped for breath. Our eyes met, and his imploring gaze begged me to help him.

The next moment, his neck twisted

. . . his feet inches from the floor and his body shaking violently like a marionette in the clutches of an invisible puppet master.

violently to the side, there was a loud crack, and the light in his eyes was extinguished as his head fell forward. I let out a cry of horror and stumbled back, shocked and frightened, yet unable to look away.

The lifeless body of Miles Morgenstern remained hovering in mid air for an instant, his dead eyes staring sightlessly into mine. Suddenly, it lurched to one side and, accompanied by a soft, strained grunt, rose towards the ceiling, flipped upside down and plunged headfirst into a large copper vat of half-set gelatine.

Transfixed, I stared at the body sinking slowly into the vat of gelatinous gloop. Chilling laughter, stifled yet clearly deranged, hissed in the air about me. I looked around the narrow attic room, but there was no one to be seen, and I took a step forward – only to be knocked roughly aside by something barging past me. I heard a sharp intake of breath and caught the faintest whiff of chemicals.

I was about to sheath my sword and hurry across to the vat when I noticed a splash of red at the tip of the blade. I touched it gingerly and inspected my fingertips. It was blood. Whatever had brushed past me must have been nicked by the blade, and I was struck by a thought.

Supernatural phantoms don't bleed; invisible he might be, but the murderer was made of flesh and blood. It wasn't a ghost or ghoul I was after. It was a person – an evil monster, maybe, but a person nonetheless.

Upending the vat, I pulled the body of Miles Morgenstern free and turned him over. I cleared the claggy gelatine from his nose and mouth with fumbling fingers, hoping against hope that the poor man might still be alive. But as I'd feared, his neck was broken. In the grip of the invisible phantom, he'd never stood a chance. I reached forward and closed his bulging eyes.

Behind me, I heard the sound of footsteps

echoing round the stairwell. I jumped to my feet, quickly left the garret and hurtled down the stairs in hot pursuit, reaching the hallway at the bottom of the building just in time to see the front door swing shut. The phantom was getting away.

'Oh, no you don't, Dean Henry Dodson,' I muttered grimly through gritted teeth as I raced outside after him.

I skidded to a halt, and looked round in surprise. The snow had thickened. Huge feathery snowflakes were fluttering down now, white against a yellow-grey sky, and settling on the city below. I groaned, my breath billowing from my mouth.

Now what? I wondered as I looked up and down the snow-covered street.

Then I saw it. Pressed into the snow on the doorstep was a footprint. Then another, and another, leading off down Brazier Street in the direction of Blue Boar Lane. As I followed them, they became farther apart, and I knew that whoever was making them had broken into a run. But there was something else about the footprints. These weren't the ridged impressions of boots or shoes. No, I could see the heels, the balls and the toes of feet; unshod feet. The phantom was barefoot.

'Murderer!' I bellowed after him as I gave chase. 'Stop! Murderer! Murderer!'

At the end of Brazier Street, the footprints turned sharply left. I skidded round the corner, straight into the busy thoroughfare of Goose Market Street, to the accompaniment of whinnying horses, the grinding of slewing carriage wheels and loud, impassioned cries.

'You cretinous oaf!'

'My legs, they're trapped!'

'What in the name of all that's holy happened?'

The street was in uproar. To my right, an old woman was lying on the pavement. A passing timber cart abruptly lurched to a standstill before me as the huge brown carthorse pulling it reared up.

'Whoa, Jed! Whoa!' the driver shouted.

A loud scream went up from the far side of the street. I turned and, through the falling snow, saw a woman stagger backwards. The next moment, the man to her right bent double and crumpled up in a heap. Beyond them, several passers-by went sprawling as the invisible phantom barged them aside.

I set off in pursuit and, as I reached the far end of the street, I saw the footprints disappearing round the corner. Blinking away the snowflakes that clung to my eyelashes and pulling my coalstack hat low over my eyes, I careered after him.

Skidding and sliding on the newly settled snow, I turned the corner into Blue Boar Lane. The snow was falling thicker than ever, with a good two inches underfoot. Ahead of me, something curious was happening to the invisible figure. Not only could I see his footprints, but now the falling snow was giving the phantom a ghostly outline as he ran through the flakes.

Reaching the corner of Blood Alley, the phantom turned to see if he was still being pursued, and from two hundred yards away, I found myself staring at the same hideous, inhuman face I'd glimpsed at the window of the lock-up. There was the one disembodied eye, the side of a grimacing mouth, and a strip of cheek, all disconnected, as if the face of Henry Dodson was slowly being reassembled.

The grisly apparition disappeared into Blood Alley. Like a wounded animal going to ground, the phantom was heading for his lair. I arrived at the lock-up on Blood Alley moments later, to find the door swinging on its hinges.

With a soft *swish*, I drew the sword from my cane, and raised it before me as I stepped cautiously inside the gloomy lock-up. Dean

Henry Dodson might, by some arcane powers of the occult or infernal alchemy, have cloaked himself in invisibility, but unlike his other victims I was armed and prepared to fight.

Just as my eyes were adjusting to the gloom, there was a small click and a sudden blinding flash, accompanied by the acrid tang of sulphur. In the next instant, something hard and blunt struck me on the side of the head.

There was a moment of searing pain. Then nothing . . .

CHAPTER
12

I don't know how long I remained uncon-
scious. A few minutes? A couple of
hours? What I do know is that when I came
round, the lock-up was stiflingly hot and
bathed in a crimson glow.

I was sitting, slumped in a high-backed
chair, my hands and feet bound tightly by
thick ropes. What a fool I'd been to enter
the phantom's lair instead of retreating to
Hibernian Yard and reporting everything to
Inspector Clackett and the city constabulary.

But then would they have believed me? I
scarcely believed it myself. An invisible professor committing murders all over town . . .

'Ah, so you're awake, Mr Grimes,' came a rasping voice from over by the blazing fire, and I gasped as I saw a large, gleaming flask rise up from the nearby workbench, tip up shakily and a stream of liquid pour down into a bubbling vat below. Noxious vapours rose up in dense, crimson clouds. 'I think it's time we had a little chat, you and I.' The voice sounded strained and racked with pain, yet there was an underlying tone of malice.

The flask was set clumsily down and, as the clouds began to clear, I saw a filthy, white laboratory coat, high-buttoned and sleeves rolled, seemingly hovering in mid air. There were stains down the front and the material was pock-marked where splashes of caustic liquids had burned holes.

Footsteps approached and, craning my neck, I saw the laboratory coat coming nearer, though I could see no trace of either the legs or feet that might be propelling it. As it drew close, a hideous apparition emerged from the red-stained fog. I stared at the fragmented patches of face floating above me as the spectral figure moved in the flickering light. A single eye, a strand of straight, matted hair and a ghastly sheen of translucent skin . . .

'My war paint appears to be smudged. This weather has played havoc with it,' the phantom sneered, obviously delighted by the horrified look on my face.

The white coat turned away and the lock-up echoed with a shriek of raucous laughter. I was in no doubt that I was in the presence of a madman. The poisonous chemicals which, even now, were swirling round the lock-up, must have stolen his reason. Miles Morgenstern had spelled out how dangerous they were. The toxic cyanide, the numbing ether and mind-warping mercury vapour had turned Dean Henry Dodson into this raging maniac, just as they had affected poor Laurence Oliphant.

I gazed up at the oliphantypes pegged to a

clothes line that hung from the ceiling above my head. The dean must have seen me, for he reached up with an unseen hand and plucked a print down from one of the waxed cords, and held it up before my eyes.

I stared at the image incredulously. It was me, caught in the moment of stepping into the lock-up in a blinding light.

'Laurence Oliphant, the greatest painter with light the world has ever seen!' the rasping voice proclaimed. 'Pioneer of oliphantography, yet how was poor Laurence treated by the very world he sought to enrich with his creation? I'll tell you, Mr Grimes. I'll tell you!

'He was betrayed, he was belittled, and he suffered torments, Mr Grimes. Torments! . . .'

The dean's voice had risen to a deranged, high-pitched scream.

'His financial backer withdrew his support! Because when he saw oliphantypes such as this one, Mr Grimes' – my photographic image shook in front of my face – 'Crispin Blears realized that painting was dead!'

The oliphantype fluttered to the floor by my feet.

'His assistant learned all he could from him, then left like a thief in the night!' the phantom rasped, as the white coat paced back and forth in front of me. 'Miles Morgenstern stole his master's work, and then contaminated it with . . . with gelatine and eggs!'

He spat the words out with contempt.

'Even his own sister refused to help poor Laurence in his hour of need. Sitting on a fortune in gold, yet she was deaf to his desperate entreaties for help . . .'

There was a barely stifled sob in the phantom's throat, quickly replaced by a rasp of malice.

'But she'll pay, just like all the others. She'll pay for her treachery!'

The white coat paused, motionless for a moment, its sleeves crossed in contemplation.

'And then came the breakthrough – terrible, hideously painful; a torment, but also a triumph! And Albert Hoskins the chemist was unwittingly responsible. Imagine that! Stupid, money-grubbing little Albert, who adulterated the chemicals he supplied to poor Laurence to save a few miserable pennies, and by doing so caused the terrible . . . miraculous accident!

'Poor Laurence. How it burned, Mr Grimes. How it burned! And yet . . . and yet . . .'

The phantom's voice was hushed with awe.

'When the fire was out and the smoke and fumes had cleared, Laurence discovered that where the chemical compound had splashed onto him, his skin had taken on a strange translucency. There was more of the curious solution lying at the bottom of the vat, as clear and slippery as mercury . . .'

He pressed his gruesome fragmented face into mine. His breath was warm and foul.

'Mirrorskin, Mr Grimes,' he said. 'That's what Laurence called it. He mixed it with goose-fat. When applied to the human skin, it renders the wearer . . .'

'Invisible,' I breathed. 'Is that why you murdered Laurence Oliphant. For this mirrorskin?'

The phantom's deranged laugh echoed round the infernal lock-up.

'Laurence Oliphant died,' he said, 'but not in the way you think, Mr Grimes. I've kept my eye on you as you snooped into his affairs. I was there in the house, giving you and your pretty little friend, Tilly, the run-around; and then in Centennial Park, upending that ridiculous contraption. But nothing you did has done Clarissa any good, I saw to that. She will hang for the murder of her brother, just as I planned!

'You see, when Laurence discovered mirrorskin, he had some fun, I don't mind admitting it. Passing freely around the city undetected was exhilarating. He helped himself to chemicals from Albert Hoskins' warehouse, he stole a pedigree boarhound from the kennels of Lord Riverhythe's estate; he pushed pedlars into canals, washerwomen into horse troughs and even slashed pompous Sir Crispin Blears' cack-handed portrait of Lady Sarah Poultney as the goddess Diana with a fencing sword!

'But then, as the pain persisted, the torments grew; headaches like needles through the eyes, voices taunting in the head. Laurence became more focused. He invited his mentor to his studio, and showed him his miraculous mirrorskin – two precious jars of the stuff – expecting the dean to be amazed. But instead of praising poor Laurence, the dean, his mentor, his hero, turned on him and told him that he was mad!

'Laurence Oliphant, mad?' the phantom screeched incredulously, crossing the room and standing behind my chair. I could feel his rasping breath on my cheek.

'So Dean Henry Dodson had to die! Laurence killed him with a sword thrust through the heart. He died without a whimper, and in that moment Laurence Oliphant died too . . .

'And I saw what I had become, Mr Grimes, through my torments. I had become a god! A god, I tell you! And how does the venerable bard put it? *As flies to wanton boys are we to th' gods, they kill us for their sport . . .*'

So I had been quite wrong, I realized. This crazed phantom before me was not Dean Henry Dodson! It was none other than Laurence Oliphant himself. Clarissa Oliphant's brother had not been murdered as everyone had been led to believe. Instead, he was the murderer, killing his tutor in cold blood, then setting off to avenge himself on those he saw as his enemies, and leaving a trail of death and destruction in his wake.

Now he had captured me. I was in the grip of a madman.

'I'd been boiling up a solution of the most caustic of chemicals; ammonium citrate and potassium ferricyanide, nitric and sulphuric acids . . . the same solution you have noticed bubbling in the vat as we speak, Mr Grimes,' Laurence added, laughing unpleasantly. 'Normally, I use such a formula to clean my metal photographic plates, but on that day, I decided to use it to eradicate the existence of Dean Henry Dodson, once and for all.

'I exchanged my clothes for his, then tipped the whole vat over him. And as the corrosive chemicals destroyed his features, I left the lock-up. Laurence Oliphant was dead, and in his place I had unleashed an avenging god on the city.

'I visited the university and faked the dean's departure note. I lured Crispin Blears from his opulent mansion and dispatched him quickly under the wheels of a post coach. At first, I was infuriated to have lost the cape, yet it proved fortuitous, since it seemed to confirm that Henry Dodson, rather than myself, had been involved in the death. Next, I decided to teach Albert Hoskins a lesson. He would learn precisely what it was like to be involved in an explosion. I clubbed the simple fool over the head and tossed matches into his warehouse.' He chuckled. 'The whole lot went up like a giant Roman candle. And then there was Miles Morgenstern . . . '

The phantom's rasping voice was close to my ear.

'But then, you know all about that, don't you, Mr Grimes?' he said, his voice soft and lulling. 'I'll teach you to meddle in my affairs.'

I looked desperately around that hellish lock-up as I fought against the ropes that bound me.

'I have suffered the torments of hell,' whispered the phantom. 'Now it is your turn, Barnaby Grimes.'

The pungent stench of sea-coal smoke and scorched chemicals made my eyes water and caught in my throat. There were splashes of a thick, viscous liquid on the floor at my feet, and the ornate brass gas lamp which jutted from the wall was ablaze.

A length of crimson silk had been wrapped round the lamp's mantle and glass cowl. It dulled the glare of the gaslight, its muted light casting the whole room in a hellish red glow. It shone on the low, flaking ceiling, on the planks of wood nailed across the single window, and on rows of portraits pinned to the walls and hanging from the clothes line above my head.

There were men and women. Old and young. A scrivener with a long quill and inky fingers. A butcher in a spattered apron with a dead rabbit raised in one hand. A milkmaid, a river-tough, a chimney-sweep's young lad ... They all gazed down at me in that crimson light, like the lost souls of the damned.

To my left, a splintered bench ran the length of the room, a sink at its centre and three large zinc trays beside it. Shelves, bowing under the weight of glass bottles of dark chemicals and glittering powders, lined the wall above it. To my right were two worm-eaten cupboards and a rickety table, its warped top overflowing with equipment. Scalpels, shears and a paper guillotine; bottles of ink and goosefeather quills; a magnifying glass, a cracked clay pipe, and a towering stack of paper that leaned against a box-shaped contraption with brass hinges and a glass top ...

Directly in front of me was the huge vat, set upon a tripod, its pungent contents bubbling furiously over a white-hot furnace. Thick clouds of crimson steam poured over the side of the cauldron and spilled out across the floor, writhing and squirming as they snaked towards me.

The toxic red steam coalesced and began to wind itself around my ankles, my calves, my knees. It burned my nostrils and stung my eyes. My head swam; my lungs were on fire. The heat made my skin prickle, and the noxious fumes left me gasping for breath as I fought desperately to free myself from the ropes that bound my hands and feet.

Just then, I felt a hand grasping my throat, pulling me out of the chair and forward onto my knees. A second hand grabbed the back of my head and thrust it forward until my face was inches above the bubbling liquid in the vat.

'Oh, how it burns, Barnaby Grimes,' the phantom's sinister voice hissed, before rising to a high-pitched crescendo. 'How it burns . . .'

I was trapped, bound hand and foot, and with a madman forcing my face into a vat of corrosive chemicals. There was only one thing I could do, so I did it.

'Help!' I screamed, at the top of my lungs. 'HELP!'

'In Blood Alley,' the phantom sneered, 'nobody can hear you scream!'

He pressed my face closer to the seething liquid in the vat. He wanted to destroy me the way he'd destroyed Dean Henry Dodson. The steam burned my lips. My eyes felt as if they were on fire.

'HELP!' I bellowed again. '*HELP!*'

All at once, the lock-up trembled with the impact of a colossal blow at the door. The phantom froze. Another blow came, together with the sound of splitting wood. The hinges gave way and the door abruptly slammed back hard against the inside wall as a massive Moravian boarhound burst snarling into the room and leaped at the white coat.

'Kaiser!' I gasped. 'Kaiser, it's you.'

The phantom screamed as Kaiser sank his

'In Blood Alley,' the phantom sneered, 'nobody can hear you scream!'

teeth into an invisible leg and shook it violently. The white coat flailed in the air as it toppled over. The phantom slammed back against the red-hot metal of the vat, and cried out with a mixture of terror and pain. The vat tilted, sending its contents sloshing over the side and into the furnace flames. They ignited at once, and with a loud wumph the whole vat was suddenly engulfed in a ball of fire.

'Kaiser!' I screamed, desperately flinging myself away from the flames.

I landed heavily on the floor, the burning liquid from the vat spreading across the stone flags towards me as the screams of the phantom filled the air.

All at once, I felt something tugging at my ankles and found myself being pulled across the floor, away from the seething vat and lapping flames. I looked down to see Kaiser, his great jaws clamped round the ropes that bound my feet, dragging me backwards, out of the room.

Above my head, the shelves and cupboards were beginning to smoulder and the splintered bench was ablaze, while the oliphantypes pegged to the clothes line burst into flames, one by one; the scrivener, the butcher, the milkmaid, the river-tough and the chimneysweep's lad, staring back at me as their images blackened and curled.

All at once, my spine cracked and my head bounced painfully down as the great boarhound dragged me over the door frame and onto the snowy cobbles outside. Several residents of Blood Alley had already emerged from nearby lock-ups and now came to my aid. As a burly mog-skinner cut the ropes that bound me, there was a massive explosion. The front of the lock-up blew out and the roof collapsed. Flames, fifty foot high, hissed as the thick snowflakes fluttered down into them. And out of the wreckage stumbled a spectral figure, his stained white coat ablaze. He staggered forwards, slipping on the snow-covered cobbles, and tumbled heavily to the ground.

'Over 'ere!' a counterfeiter shouted urgently, as he struggled to tear off the figure's blazing coat. He wrenched one sleeve free, then the other, ripped the buttons off and rolled the body onto its front. He tossed the coat aside. Flames danced over the curious, transparent body beneath. 'Quick!' he bellowed. 'Water, now!'

Two bootleggers came running, a man and a woman, each with a bucket sloshing at their side. They raised them as one and sluiced the water over the burning figure. The flames were doused in an instant and, as the water trickled down over the blistered body, it washed away the mirrorskin, revealing the figure beneath.

I crouched down and, taking hold of a shoulder, rolled the body over. The snowmelt and water trickled down his face, washing away the last of the chemicals that had made him invisible. The face that appeared looked remarkably calm and, apart from the red scar and singed hair, I felt I was looking at the person Laurence Oliphant had once been: a quiet, mild-mannered man, studious and sympathetic to others . . .

His eyelids flickered and opened, and he gazed up at me through clear green eyes. Beside me, Kaiser crouched down and licked my hand. Laurence smiled weakly, grimacing slightly as he struggled with the pain that gripped his burnt body. His eyes widened and he grasped my arm.

'Please,' he said, his voice husky and faltering. 'Tell Clarissa . . . I'm sorry . . .'

There was a soft rattle in his throat and his head fell back. His eyes closed. Kaiser whimpered and pawed at the body, but in vain. This time there was no doubt, no room for error, no chance of a reprieve.

Laurence Oliphant was dead.

*

Inspector Clackett listened to my story with rapt attention, occasionally raising a hand to stop me mid flow as he jotted something down in his notebook. When I was done, he climbed to his feet and paced back and forth across the small room, glancing up at the sinister death masks on the walls. He began talking quickly, quietly, as if to himself.

'A deranged scientist, driven mad by the toxic chemicals of his trade? After all, it has happened before – with the Mad Hatter murders of '47. Four murders this time, and Laurence Oliphant had both the motive and the opportunity for each of them. And by faking his own death, he threw us all off the scent . . .'

He paused and turned to me, as if seeing me for the first time.

'Well, Mr Grimes, I've got to hand it to you,' he said. 'You seem to have cracked the case. 'Course, I don't know about these here jars of so-called mirrorskin you mentioned. By the time that lock-up fire was finally put out, there was barely a trace of anything left inside.' He stroked his hooked nose thoughtfully. 'But the rest of the story certainly stands up. After all, Miss Oliphant can hardly have murdered her brother when he didn't in fact die until the fire, which happened when she was safely locked up in Whitegate Model Prison . . .'

'So?' I said.

'So, Miss Oliphant is free to go,' the inspector said, thrusting his hand out before me. I shook it warmly. 'And she's got you to thank for it,' he added. 'If it hadn't been for you, Barnaby Grimes . . .' He paused, and pointed to the death masks on the wall. 'I only hope she appreciates all you've done for her.'

She did. The following morning I paid Clarissa Oliphant a visit. Despite being in deep mourning for her brother, she seemed to be bearing up well, and I was pleased to note that the brief spell in prison hadn't seemed to do any lasting damage to her indomitable spirit. As Tilly ushered me into the drawing room, the duelling governess cast her fencing manual aside and leaped up from her chair.

'Mr Grimes,' she said. 'Barnaby. I was hoping you'd drop by. I have something for you.' She reached into the side pocket of the crisp, black jacket she was wearing and pulled out a small pouch, which she pressed into my hands. 'A reward for your troubles.'

I was about to protest that I hadn't done it for the money, but she patted my hands.

'You've earned it, Barnaby, my lad,' she said, and smiled. 'And you might be pleased to know that I've given Tilly the rest of the day off.'

Back in my attic rooms that night, I lay out the contents of the pouch on my table. There were nineteen of them in all – small, round and slightly charred gold sovereigns, part of the hoard recovered from a strongbox in

Laurence Oliphant's lock-up. There had been twenty of them, but having commissioned a wheelboard from Will Farmer's blacksmith friend, bought Tilly a new bonnet from *Gosney and Daughter*, Will a new poacher's waistcoat, taken Molly, Will and Tilly out for an oyster supper *and* treated us all to a box at the Alexandra Hippodrome, I'd had just enough left for one more thing . . .

I slipped the remaining nineteen sovereigns back into the pouch and slid it under the mattress. Kaiser lifted his head and looked at me, his thick eyebrows raised and his brand-new collar and nameplate glistening.

'Nineteen gold sovereigns,' I told him. 'A small fortune for the likes of you and me, and I've got big plans for us both.'

Little did I know then that Kaiser's former owner, the new Lord Riverhythe, was going to cross swords with me in the Templeton wing of the city museum on the very night the prophecy of Pharaoh Akanaten III was due to come true, unleashing a horror on the city few could imagine.

But that, as they say, is another story . . .